SRUSHTI KULKARNI

THE TIMEKEEPER AND THE 25ᵀᴴ HOUR

BLUEROSE PUBLISHERS
India | U.K.

Copyright © Srushti Kulkarni 2024

All rights reserved by author. No part of this publication may be reproduced, stored in a retrieval system or transmitted in any form or by any means, electronic, mechanical, photocopying, recording or otherwise, without the prior permission of the author. Although every precaution has been taken to verify the accuracy of the information contained herein, the publisher assumes no responsibility for any errors or omissions. No liability is assumed for damages that may result from the use of information contained within.

BlueRose Publishers takes no responsibility for any damages, losses, or liabilities that may arise from the use or misuse of the information, products, or services provided in this publication.

For permissions requests or inquiries regarding this publication, please contact:

BLUEROSE PUBLISHERS
www.BlueRoseONE.com
info@bluerosepublishers.com
+91 8882 898 898
+4407342408967

ISBN: 978-93-5989-857-5

Cover design: Shivam
Typesetting: Namrata Saini

First Edition: February 2024

Contents

Grandparent's Letter 1
Cerulean Essence 17
Flummoxed 30
World of Time 47
Exploring more 66
Royal Pine 66 79
What's the plan? 95
Decoction factory 106
The Card of Intimation 116
The Battle begins 125
Vault 20:07 131
The Cryptogram 143
The Exact Story 154

Grandparent's Letter

'That is unusual. I have never seen this kind of thing in my life. Have you?' asked Mr Parikh, surprisingly, to his eleven-year-old daughter, Avni, as they were busy clicking photos of a bird perched on a tree in their building's garden. It was a pleasant Sunday morning with partly cloudy sky since it was the rainy season and a light drizzle had started by the time the father-daughter duo clicked different photos of the magnificent bird. Indeed, the bird was unusual, though small, but with pink colour and beautiful blue stripes on its feathers. It was a silent bird with no chirping at all. It just looked here and there with its bright black eyes as though giving a perfect pose for a photoshoot. It kept moving back and forth frequently, on the same branch it was perching upon.

'No, dad. I haven't. Even I am surprised- oh no! That is not perfect photo dad. The angle should be brilliant for such a beguiling bird,' replied Avni, a short and black-haired eleven-year-old girl, not good at anything except photography and a bit of mind reading. She had dark brown eyes just like her father and liked to do only three things – pondering over her future, photography and reading other people's minds. The third hobby was quite unusual in people but that was considered as an inborn talent in Avni and her twin brother Rohan and appreciated by many.

The Parikh family lived in Mumbai and included five members- Mr and Mrs. Parikh and the three children,

Akriti (ninth grader), Rohan and Avni (the twins). Not forgetting their 'sixth member'- Tulip, a cute little brownish-orange cat, liked by all in the Parikh family.

Though they were a middle-class family living in a flat in Golden High Rise Co-operative housing society, Parikh's' relatives used to be jealous of them as they stayed in a perfect surrounding with nature's beauty at its peak. A beautiful garden with lush green grass and mango trees and along with that, the building gave a pretty view of half brown, half green mountains and most importantly the green grass growing taller every day, could be seen at the bottom of the mountain. But this was all at the backside of the building which could be seen from the kitchen side balcony. On the front side, as people went outside the large gate of the building, one could see a long road which almost gave the feeling of a highway. On the other side of the road there were a few shops for daily requirements like grocery and general stores. The two twins Avni and Rohan always enjoyed going for a long bicycle ride to bring their school things. They just needed an excuse for going out and travelling a few kilometres up to the stationery shop.

Meanwhile Avni and her dad were still busy with that bird, instructing each other over their mistakes. 'Alright, you may only take the brilliant angle, yeah,' said Mr Parikh with a bold look and a bit of disappointment for not taking a good shot, straightening his big square shaped spectacles.

'I am only good at photography, dad. At least in this I can use my brain to get a flawless shot. Isn't it?' said Avni with a frown on her face. The drizzle had increased by that time and she felt a few droplets of rain rolling down her cheeks.

'No, my child. Even I was not good at most of the things as a child, still you see I have completed my MBA in Finance and Marketing and I am earning quite well, right!' said her father with a wide grin. 'You are forgetting one more talent which you and Rohan possess, reading people's mind,' he added, nodding his head. The tall father figure was very sweet natured towards everyone and would never let anyone feel low about themselves. He ensured everybody always remained happy, no matter whatever issues one faces. But he was a bit protective about things since he always instructed his family not to waste anything and use everything they had, properly.

'Yeah dad, you always inspire us to move on. Oh! It will start raining heavily. We should go. We haven't got umbrellas!' said Avni and she ran away quickly, back in the building with her left hand covering her head, and her jacket had become a bit wet. Her dad too followed with the camera in his hands. He was wiping the camera with his fingers, fearing it will not function properly the next time they went for clicking photos.

They waited outside the lift for it to return to the ground floor. Meanwhile they met the secretary of the building who was the strangest person ever born in the world. Always strict about following rules. 'Excuse me, Mr Raghav Parikh! You haven't yet given the house maintenance cheque of this month. How forgetful. I will not spare you. Give it today itself, understood?' said the grumpy, loud voiced and *'by mistake elected secretary,'* K.O. Verma, though no one knew his full name and even if anyone dared to ask about his name, he used to penalise them with five hundred rupees. So, the members from the building had warned each other not to ask him about the name. They had assumed that he probably did not like his name.

'Oh god! How many times will you forget Mr Verma? Today is the 14th of June. The date of giving cheque is the 21st. Isn't it?' said Mr Parikh annoyingly. Avni frowned and closed her eyes for a second and waited for the lift to arrive.

'Mmm…yeah…sorry I forgot. You may continue with your work Mr Parikh,' said K.O. Verma and left the place where they were standing and went marching outside the building, probably to give useless instructions to other people who met him on the way.

Avni and her dad reached their home, on the third floor.

The doorbell rang. Mrs Parikh opened the door and raised her eyebrows and said- 'I thought you would not return for at least another hour,' giving a small grin.

It was now raining heavily and it made a huge splashing noise over the window which answered Mrs Parikh why the two were back earlier than usual from their favourite recreational activity.

The Parikh family lived in a three bedroom-hall-kitchen house with a small kitchen side balcony. The entrance door was on the right side and there could be seen a large living room with attractive furniture. Sponge painted walls and a sofa on the left with a beautiful small table in front consisting of three-dimensional painting; if seen from the left one could see a waterfall and from the right, a lush green forest. There was a small passage inside, kitchen on the right with a nice dining table and three rooms on the left with three huge wood brown-coloured doors.

Avni and her father came inside checking the camera and phone if they were still working and sat on the chairs kept near the door.

'Mom since I am wet, can you please brew me a cup of coffee. I think dad too will have it. Right dad?' said Avni, removing her half-wet socks. Her mom went right into the kitchen nodding and Avni looked around the living room for her twin brother and her elder sister. Akriti and Rohan both were busy reading books and their eyes were wide open without giving a single blink. Avni saw that Akriti was reading a mystery book and Rohan was absorbed in a magical-verse book which was his favourite genre. He did not even realise until his mother shouted at him that his cup of coffee was dropping down on the floor, as he held the cup in a tilted position.

'I think they are very much engrossed in the books,' said Mr Parikh giving a short laugh to which the two gave annoying expressions and again got busy reading. 'Hmm…let them do it dad. But we enjoyed clicking photos, isn't it?' said Avni and went to meet her cat Tulip who was sitting in the corner of the room hiding behind the sofa. She seemed to be annoyed with the loud noise of the heavy rains which grew deeper.

By lunch time everyone gathered at the table, cracking jokes and laughing at each other merrily. The rain had stopped but the clouds were still there and it was a bit dark hinting at another round of heavy rains.

'Hey mom, what is on the menu for today? Since it's Sunday, any special dish…' said Akriti in a happy tone. She was a sincere girl, always conscious about studying. Very specific about her daily routine as she would set up a to-do list every day in the morning and plan what she will do for the whole day. She wore a sincere look on her face just like her mother but equally playful and amiable with others.

'I have made *spinach parathas*, *khichdi* and *kadhi* for lunch. Couldn't prepare much since I feel a bit tired today. For the desert we have *rasgullas*,' replied Mrs Parikh smiling at her children.

'That's more than enough, mom,' said Akriti with a big smile. The children always felt that their mother was very dedicated towards her work and there was a kind element in her which they liked a lot but were afraid of her too as once she started scolding for their mistakes, nobody would stop her. Mrs Parikh was a thin and not so tall lady. She always tied her hair in a bun and liked to cook different dishes.

'Nice, I like that. I think I am going to enjoy it,' said Rohan, shaking his head and looking at the dishes which his mother was bringing one by one. Rohan always liked to crack jokes and make everyone laugh and apart from this he had a special liking for discussing supernatural powers and mysterious fictional characters from movies and books. Also, he shared the same special talent of reading other people's minds as his twin sister Avni could.

'I have only twenty minutes to eat since after lunch I am going to make notes of my next chapter of Chemistry. You know it is about the *atomic structure*. I feel it's a bit difficult but I think, I can manage well,' said Akriti, serving her plate as fast as she could. 'I have to eat as fast as I can,' she muttered.

Tulip, their cat started meowing again and made strange noises, this time not for the rain but for lunch. 'Wait my dear, I will give you cat food and milk,' said Mrs Parikh serving her with the same. The cat started pouncing here and there out of happiness and then sat at one place looking into the bowl which had been offered to her.

'Tomorrow, we have an essay writing competition, dad, in our school. Should I participate or not? I mean, I am not interested but just for the sake of fun…' asked Avni putting a large piece of rasgulla into her mouth. 'Haven't they collected the list of names and details before, participants name, I mean,' interrupted Mrs Parikh looking at Avni questioningly.

'No, that was a very quick announcement, made on Friday that too in the last lecture,' said Rohan. 'I am participating this time.'

'See, you should always be inquisitive to learn, so in my opinion, Avni, you should participate, right Anjali?' said Mr Parikh to Mrs Parikh, expecting a 'yes' from her.

'Yeah, sure,' replied Mrs Parikh. The rain again splashed on the window and a lot of mist had gathered. It was thundering loudly. Meanwhile Akriti went to her room after she finished with her lunch, for making notes with widened and frightened eyes as she felt a bit scared of loud thunder. But the discussion about other things continued among the rest and Tulip went mad listening to the rain.

'Avni, what if the topic for essay writing is my favourite character- *Master Jack*, from the book, *The Mysterious Time Stopper?*' asked Rohan with gleaming eyes, looking into the ceiling.

'Oh, not at all. According to me the topic should be- 'What if there was a 25th hour of time?' replied Avni, thumping the table. 'Or about reading people's minds…that would also do, isn't it Rohan?'

'I don't think they will give any topics of our interest, some tough topics will be given, probably,' said Rohan with a serious expression and putting rasgulla in his mouth.

The twins always liked to talk about things related to time, supernatural powers and much more. At times they plotted stories and amused themselves with the same. Mr and Mrs Parikh would be surprised at their behaviour many times but did not pay much attention.

'Hey, I remembered from writing, what about Grandpa and Granny? They did not write any letter to us since many days, like they usually do,' asked Avni with a thump on the table, this time it was louder. Their paternal grandpa and granny used to stay in Ahmedabad, looking after their ancestral property. Every time they sent a letter to Mumbai asking about how things are. They liked the traditional way of contacting people and rarely used mobiles.

'No, we didn't receive any letter yet. Even I am waiting for it,' said Mr Parikh pulling Rohan's hands off as he was trying to eat a third piece of rasgulla. 'Oh dad, let me eat,' said Rohan with a frown.

'Don't let him take that piece. Enough Rohan. You are done with your dessert. Go and study now, you both. If we receive the letter, we will let you know,' said Mrs Parikh collecting the desert bowls.

'What I feel is, this time Grandpa may call our parents to Ahmedabad for some work,' muttered Avni to Rohan in a low voice as they headed back to their rooms. She had got an intuition.

After some time, Avni tried hard to concentrate on her book but in vain. Rohan pretended to study for ten minutes or so and then roamed around the house doing nothing.

It was not more than half an hour when Avni started becoming restless, not willing to study any more. She was reading a lesson from History regarding the stone age, ancient times, and stuff. She was wondering how people used to live in those days without any facilities and most importantly, social media without which today's generation cannot stay. She was a bit disappointed that there were no electronic devices at that time.

The rain had stopped, but there was a lot of mist on the windows and the sky was half clear. Then she got up from her place only to see what Akriti was doing. She peeped in her Chemistry textbook and saw that her elder sister had been writing important points. She had put up empty sticky notes on blank sheets.

Suddenly they heard Tulip making strange noises and both of them jumped at once. They went to see what made the cat make such noise. Rohan was teasing the cat. He was saying – 'you are afraid of the rain, isn't it? Tulip is afraid.'

'Stop it, Rohan. Come here Tulip, you are a good cat,' said Akriti cuddling the cat in her hands. Meanwhile they sat outside doing some time pass with the cat.

After a few minutes when Tulip went to doze off in her 'cat house', the trinity and their mother had a discussion on the upcoming first unit tests in July. Though this topic was not of any interest to Avni but this time she too was a bit nervous. She always saw her elder sister hard-pressed with her books even more during the exams, so gradually she was developing a different lookout about her exams and studies, not really, but then she was concerned about her mom who would be more than tensed for the twins and their marks. Her twin brother was almost on similar lines with his sister and this time both participated in this conversation. Mr Parikh had been to nearby shop for repairing his laptop after lunch and he had told Mrs Parikh before going that he would not return until it would get repaired.

'I have prepared a timetable for the upcoming exams. Though our school started recently after the summer holidays, the exams approach us with a bullet train's speed and we end up thinking about what will happen to our marks…then horrible results…and stuff,' said Akriti with a stern expression. 'I can make one for you both, twinnies…' and they all laughed at her saying 'twinnies'. Tulip growled as she was dozing off and the laughter disturbed her.

'Hmm…even we plan to study this time,' said the twins simultaneously. 'And that too sincerely,' they added further.

'Is it? Hope so you remember your words. You both,' said Mrs Parikh smiling at them as she was preparing a list of groceries to be purchased sitting at the kitchen table. The twins nodded their heads together. But some noise distracted Rohan and his ears were concentrating on that. Someone in their building had been playing piano loudly. He smiled at the sweet tuned music and kept shaking his head at the tune. He was no more listening to the conversation. He saw that Avni too was grooving to the tune.

'See, mom, just a few seconds ago they were talking about studying sincerely and now they are enjoying the piano tune. They get distracted so easily,' said Akriti. 'This will not—

And the doorbell rang, Mrs Parikh went to open it, giving a look at the two shaking heads who were busy listening to the music.

Mr Parikh came in with a very angry mood which was quite rare to see. 'This fat headed secretary Mr Verma. I don't know how he became the secretary of our building…' he said, moving his fists in anger.

'What happened Raghav?' asked Mrs Parikh out of concern to which he replied that the secretary met him and started giving instructions about how to use an electronic device like laptop easily and properly. That speech of his went on for twenty minutes. If Mr Parikh had not listened to his 'bank of instructions', the secretary would have probably penalised him. Then he said things like 'nobody complains about him, how did he get elected, I shall complain one day…'

'But that's not fair dad,' said Akriti, coming out only to find out that Tulip had woken up and jumped upon her, meowing.

'I know dear. But cannot help,' said Mr Parikh and sat on the sofa opening the laptop.

At around half past five during tea time everyone once again gathered at the kitchen table. Mrs Parikh had prepared tea for themselves and chocolate milk for the children with some fruit cake pastries and homemade cookies for the evening snacks. Mr Parikh was reciting the letter sent by his father. He took a sip of tea from the mug and read loudly-

Hello dears,

Hope everything is fine at your end in Mumbai. Here in Ahmedabad, it's raining heavily. How are Akriti, Avni and Rohan? It's been a long time we have seen them-

Mr Parikh looked up from his spectacles and then at the children giving a short laugh because of the last sentence he had read- 'It's been a long time we have seen them.' They had met just two months ago and they always tried to be funny in some or the other way, hence mentioned it considering that everyone will laugh.

He continued with the letter-

There is some property related work here for which we need your help, Raghav. Please come here and do the needful. Hoping to see you on '17th June', take the flight and come here flying! Loads of love to our three little lovelies.

P.S – We forgot to mention before, the work might take two to three days to complete, plan your leave accordingly, Raghav.

Mr and Mrs Parikh (THE SENIORS)

He kept the letter on the table and the twins laughed at the thing which grandpa had written mentioning separately about themselves as 'seniors', at the end. Avni had taken a large piece of the pastry into her mouth and so her brother and could not laugh that loudly and Rohan muttered with pastry in his mouth- 'Good gracious Avni, your prediction was right. Grandpa has called them to Ahmedabad.'

'So, we need to go there, Anjali. On the 17th. I should book a flight now,' said Mr Parikh trying to sip tea from the mug.

'Yeah. You need to take three days off,' said Mrs Parikh, pursing her lips.

'Hmm…grandpa mentioned it in the P.S,' said Rohan giggling.

Akriti listened to the whole thing but probably absent-mindedly as she had to take down her notes for Physics subject now.

'What if the flight gets cancelled?' asked Avni with widened eyes as if she was willing to crack a joke. 'I mean it's the rainy season, will you get a flight, perfectly scheduled, without any issues?'

'Why do you always say the opposite? Can't you think positive?' asked Mrs Parikh with a displeased expression to which Mr Parikh replied- 'It is alright, Anjali. She is a child.'

'Thanks dad,' said Avni taking a sip of chocolate milk from her mug, smiled at her father and then rolled her eyes over to her mother and saw that Mrs Parikh gave a loud sigh out of irritation. Rohan enjoyed the small friendly talk between Avni and their dad as he took her side and then put his head into the book which he had read in the morning with his cup of chocolate milk in one hand. Mrs Parikh said, still looking a bit annoyed, 'I hope this time you don't drop the milk on the floor like you did with your coffee in the morning.'

'No- I won't,' said Rohan with a careless kind of an expression.

Akriti was not that interested with their short talks and was busy writing as soon as she finished with her pastry and cookie, planning about her physics chapter on *gravitation*.

With a lot of struggle Mr Parikh somehow managed to book a flight to Ahmedabad for 17th of June. It was in the morning at eight o' clock.

Mrs Parikh seemed to be in a hurry the evening before 17th. She told her children- 'Tomorrow Neha will arrive in the morning before we leave. She will look after you all. Ok?'

'Fine' was the reply from the children nodding their heads.

'You all will behave properly. Ok?'

'Fine'

'We are returning on the 20th, in the evening. Ok?'

'Fine'

'Do not trouble your aunt Neha at all. I don't want any complaint, especially you two, Rohan and Avni. Ok?

'Fine'

'Oh god. What is this word "fine" you both are repeating, every time I say anything?' said Mrs Parikh putting a packet of snacks into her big orange coloured handbag.

'Mumma, you are just going for three days and you look so tense as if you are going out of the planet, somewhere else in the universe,' said Avni.

'Mars planet, I suppose,' said Rohan with a broad grin and the look which his mother gave him made him put his head into the same book again.

'Since the last one month he has been reading the same book. I think you aren't able to understand the story. Is it bro?' said Akriti scribbling something in her physics notebook to which her brother gave a not-so-funny-statement look and she giggled and went to help her mother in packing, closing her notebook.

Mrs Parikh had finished packing after a few minutes with the help of Akriti and by that time Mr Parikh had arrived from his office. Luckily it wasn't raining much which comforted Mrs Parikh that probably the next day when they were leaving, the same weather should be helpful but she feared the heavy rains at the same time.

At half past eight they were having dinner. Mrs Parikh had prepared *veg soup, jeera fried rice* and *dal.* Tulip was sitting quietly, leaning on the fridge door, and licking her face. She did not show much interest in eating her cat food and looked as if she was unhappy with something, but nobody paid attention to her except Akriti and rest everyone was busy with their dinner. Mrs Parikh also kept instructing the twins on their behaviour. She constantly repeated saying – 'You both trouble my sister once and all your fun activities will be banned.' The twins just nodded absent-mindedly.

After finishing dinner, the kids were trying to finish their homework and at the same time they discussed meeting their maternal aunt Mrs Neha Dave (Mrs Parikh's elder sister), the next day.

'I am excited to meet our aunt,' said Avni, trying hard to finish the homework. Akriti was about to finish her English homework only when she noticed that by mistake, she had written her aunt's name in the answer instead of the character from the story- *Aunt Alice* from her literature textbook.

'Yeah, she is such a nice person,' said Rohan pushing Avni's notebook aside as he tried to adjust himself and his Geography book on the common study table. 'We will leave for school at 8:40 am, before that she will come, I suppose.'

'Hmm…mom and dad are leaving very early for the airport. I think we should try finishing our homework as fast as we can. Tomorrow we will try to wake up at six o' clock, not half past six, so that we may get time to chit chat with our aunt,' said Akriti, now opening her Maths text book. Avni looked at how her elder sister was taking down the books one by one and trying to finish homework. She too tried to finish Geography assignment unwillingly after her English homework was done.

'Avni, you have written wrong spelling of rivers, correct them,' said Rohan pointing out the mistake. She hit her head with pencil and with heavy and sleepy eyes she corrected her mistakes. They all finished the homework and went to sleep. Nobody was awake, even after a loud thunder, though it was not raining. The weather had become very dark, but the Parikh family was in deep sleep to wake up early the next day.

Cerulean Essence

'Good morning, Akriti,' said Avni rubbing her eyes and switching off the alarm clock with half closed eyes as she woke up at sharp six. Her sister too woke up and replied 'GM' as she felt too lazy to say the full sentence. Rohan also came out of his room to see whether his sisters had woken up. They did not speak much until they freshened up themselves and slowly packed their bags and made their raincoats and umbrellas ready, though it was not raining on that day as had Mrs Parikh wished.

At quarter to seven Mrs Dave had arrived, only in time as it took her half an hour from her house in Mumbai to travel to her sister's house in the same city.

Mr and Mrs Parikh left early finishing their breakfast. At seven they were in the taxi. Mr Parikh got down three times to check if all the luggage was taken and Mrs Parikh kept instructing the children until the taxi went out of the gate of the building. 'Bye dear kids, I will miss you for three days,' said Mr Parikh finally getting into the taxi.

'I think for the twentieth time I am telling you, do not trouble your aunt. Ok? Now bye-bye. See you my lovelies,' said Mrs Parikh and the children waved at them.

'Let us go back, children, you did not have your breakfast. It is ten past seven, now,' said Mrs Dave looking at her watch. 'Nice to meet you aunt, we are so happy,' said

Avni smiling at her aunt as they went back to their house. 'I am also glad to meet you three,' replied Mrs Dave.

Their aunt, Mrs Neha Dave, was a very sweet hearted lady and helpful too. She had thick dark brown and long hair which she always tied in plates. She looked very similar to Mrs Parikh, her younger sister. She was equally thin like her.

They were sitting at the breakfast table and waited for their aunt to prepare something tasty. 'See, your mum told me to prepare some fruit salad, bread toasts and of course milk,' said Mrs Dave cutting apple into small pieces. 'Your school starts at nine o'clock in the morning, right?'

'Yes, we need to settle ourselves by nine and at ten minutes past nine our first lecture begins. But we need to reach there by 8:40 am,' said Akriti arranging her plate and spoon.

'Never mind, you won't be late at all, your breakfast is almost ready,' said Mrs Dave pouring the milk into three large glasses.

After few minutes she had managed to prepare the breakfast items and the children had it happily, only hesitating a bit to drink the milk.

They donned their uniforms and were ready in time. The school bus arrived at half past eight as it took ten minutes to reach the school by bus and it went off quickly as they kept waving at their aunt from the bus window.

'I hope the day goes faster. I get bored sometimes, sitting in the lectures for long,' said Avni with a frustrated tone as they now climbed the staircase of the school. 'See, its till 2:30 pm, only around five and half-hours,' said Akriti to which Rohan gave an expression as if he meant to say- 'What? Only?'

They studied in a school of Mumbai. The school building was square in shape and had four floors with classes from 1st to 12th, with staircases on both sides of ground floor. One large ground for playing and separate laboratories for Chemistry, Physics, Computer and Biology. There was one activity room where students in free lectures could try few activities of their choice. There were charts all over the school with inspiring quotes and knowledgeable stuff. One assembly hall was situated on the ground floor.

'Ok bye, Akriti, will meet you in the recess,' said Rohan as he and Avni went to their class on the second floor. Akriti had to climb one more floor as she waved at her twin brother-sister.

The twins had History as their first lecture and Avni thought, what if she sleeps midway and the teacher gives her a nice punishment, so, she tried to keep her eyes wide as the teacher taught them about ancient monuments and how they were built. Rohan thought the same as Avni so he kept noting down the points as the teacher explained them, to remain active throughout.

The girl sitting beside Avni, kept on writing down whatever their teacher explained, pages after pages, to which Avni gave weird expressions and suddenly pretended to take pencil in her hand, putting her head into the book as the teacher passed staring at her.

'Avni Parikh! Try to concentrate well, do not wander away in some other world,' shouted the teacher straightening her spectacles and the whole class turned back at Avni and she felt so embarrassed that for the next half of the lecture she listened to the teacher with utmost attention.

'Lend me your notes, afterwards,' said the friend to Avni as she saw her marking paragraphs in the book. Avni thought, that this girl wanted more notes even after writing three to four pages till now and then nodded her head in agreement.

In the recess during lunch time, the three of them met in the corridor. They were discussing about the workshop notice put up on the notice board on the second floor of the school.

'How to manage your time well, is the topic of this workshop. Seems interesting as well as useful,' said Rohan who suddenly wondered about his first unit exams.

'Time is precious. You will not know how it flies off, until you realise your mistake about doing things within time. We should not procrastinate. Isn't it Avni?' said Akriti laughing in a low tone.

'Yeah, we shouldn't,' said Avni frowning at her sister's mockery.

Something struck Rohan and he suddenly spoke- 'By the way, I remembered from time, I need a wall clock. My room clock isn't working. I think today we will go with our aunt to buy few essentials from the *Cerulean Essence Shop*....'

They were back at home after school and their aunt was much delighted to see them than she was in the morning as she would get more time to spend with her nieces and nephew now. She also told them that Mr and

Mrs Parikh had reached safely in Ahmedabad and that they would call in the evening.

Akriti and Avni were wearing a green jumper as they thought of twinning with each other and Rohan wore a dull yellow jumper, so Avni started flaunting about hers and teased Rohan for the colour of his jumper. They had brought new umbrellas for the ongoing rainy season and in the drawing room, Avni and Akriti were interested in photography, so one by one they clicked photos with new long umbrellas, showing off their stylish jumpers and shoes. But unfortunately, one pic of Akriti turned out to be horrible as it thundered loudly and she almost fell, so Rohan was teasing her in revenge.

Tulip was purring sitting in the corner and was too lazy for the whole day. She did not get up from her place at all. Mrs Dave took the cat in her hands and dropped her at a neighbour's house as they had to go out.

The weather was looking a bit dull and dark with not so heavy drizzle but still they went out to the Cerulean Essence Shop without giving a second thought about heavy rains and the twins, Avni and Rohan were willing to go cycling straight through.

'Aunt, can't we go cycling? We are wearing raincoats. We like cycling, pleeeeeeease…' said Avni who was very excited and kept jumping.

'Yeah, we love cycling and that through rains, wow!' exclaimed Rohan.

'No, you will not. Please listen to me, dear. Your mother will scold you a lot if she gets to know. By chance if you both catch cold and fever, what will I answer your mother? And personally too, I do not want you to go cycling. You will come in my car. It may start raining heavily, we cannot predict,' said Mrs Dave folding her hands, looking at the two. Akriti did not say anything, she was busy tying the lace of her shoes.

The twins were not still willing to get into the car and they kept looking at their bicycles in the parking lot, turning their heads hard, till Mrs Dave drove out of the building. The weather indicated it was really going to rain heavily and dark clouds had gathered but the sound of thunder was low. On the way to the shop, Avni thought, how nice it would be if the rains were too heavy and the school gave a long holiday! Because this had happened many a times, the news channel had announced a day or two's holiday in school due to heavy rains and the amount of happiness which she experienced was simply great. She smiled looking at the sky from the car window and soon they reached the shop.

Mrs Dave parked her car in the parking area. They all got down and approached the huge iron gate of the shop. It was just for the sake of calling it as a shop but, it was a huge store and had an iron gate.

The name of the store was written in gold and a stylish font- *CERULEAN ESSENCE*. It was a multipurpose kind of a shop. Stationery, gifts, household items and many more things were there. They had kept their umbrellas outside and at the entrance, on the door it was written as push but Avni tried to pull it, probably she was still thinking about a holiday being announced in school. Rohan asked raising his eyebrows- 'Don't you know what "push" means? Why are you trying to pull?'

Then Avni realised her mistake at which Akriti and Mrs Dave were laughing and they went inside before the twins. 'Thinking about few days off from school, eh? Due to rains…' said Rohan in a very low tone to Avni who did not look much surprised at his guess but just glanced at him and said – 'yes,' giggling. The two of them could easily recognise what they both were thinking, many a times.

The receptionist at the entrance smiled at them and said 'welcome' and she sent a sales girl with them to help with the purchase.

Cerulean Essence was quite huge from inside as well, not less than a mall. It had different sections for different items. Akriti was racing up and down the same section of stationery items, searching for pencil stand and some colour papers but she was unable to select the right one. The twins were busy in the household items section, selecting a beautiful piece of wall clock. The sales girl showed them many pieces but they did not like any.

Mrs Dave was trying to help Akriti and the twins alternatively with a big shopping trolley. A loud thunder suddenly boomed which gave a pounding in Akriti's mind and she ran towards the section where the twins were standing who were still busy choosing a wall clock but the rains outside did not bother them much. 'It's good that both of them didn't pay attention that you were scared stiff of that thunder and came running here,' said Mrs Dave to Akriti. 'Otherwise, it would have become their topic of laughter.'

'Yeah,' said Akriti who tried to pretend as if she wasn't scared of anything. 'I have managed to get a pencil stand and few colour papers, but what are you two doing. Not able to find a clock yet? Should I help?' she asked.

'Yes, sure…' was the reply.

There were many beautiful clock pieces. A red one with an attractive design of all school accessories like bag, uniform and pencils surrounding the dial. A plain greenish yellow and circular one which didn't look that impressive and a pure white, square shaped clock was kept at the top shelf. None could fit their likes. It was around 5'o clock now and they kept searching. The sales girl also got bored, showing them the same pieces again and again so she went towards some other customer, helping with the purchase.

Suddenly a boy holding some stationery items approached them from behind the stationery section and said- 'Hello, this is Robin. Robin Spencer.' He was a bit tall, with dark black hair and large dark black eyes. He was of about eleven. He was wearing a jumper which was similar to what Rohan was wearing. The three siblings and Mrs Dave looked surprised, wondering who the boy was. 'Hello, this is Rohan Parikh,' said Rohan, hesitantly, holding a clock. 'Er- how can I help you?' he asked to the new person they had just met.

'Umm…well, I just wanted to say hello. I am new in this area. I saw you enter this shop and you seem to be of my age,' replied Robin. 'As such I don't know anyone here, I am new to this whole city.'

'Where are your parents and where do you stay?' asked Mrs Dave, lucidly.

'Well, I came alone to the shop and I am finding a house in this area,' said Robin, with gleaming eyes.

Mrs Dave felt strange as he did not answer her question properly.

'Ok, let me introduce my sisters and aunt to you,' said Rohan, who seemed to be willing to make friends with him. 'This is my aunt- Mrs Neha Dave, my elder sister- Akriti and my twin- Avni,' he said pointing at everyone who were just smiling.

Mrs Dave was not willing to introduce themselves so much to the boy but Rohan had already spoken.

'Hello everyone, nice to meet you all. By the way are you buying a piece of clock, Rohan?' asked Robin curiously.

'Yes,' said Rohan absent-mindedly, looking at the beautiful gold coloured watch which the boy, Robin was wearing, in his left hand. It looked a bit different from any normal watches and Rohan smiled at him, again giving a glance at the fascinating watch. But he was unwilling to ask about the watch in his very first meet so he preferred to keep quiet.

'Oh no! I did not realise that its ten minutes past five. I am getting late. Hope so we meet again, Rohan. Bye-bye,' said the tall boy, Robin and he ran away out of sight.

Rohan was thinking about his watch, but then Avni clutched his hand and said- 'Lets continue to find a clock, if we are able to.' Rohan kept wondering about the boy and his watch and searched the second shelf. He had got a new friend now and he thought, maybe if Robin meets him the next time, he would ask him about the golden watch he wore.

After a few minutes, Avni approached Rohan, looking a bit surprised with a beautiful piece of clock in her hand. She said – 'I wonder, this timepiece wasn't there, when I went there earlier to search for one, but now…'

The clock she had brought in just now, was simply magnificent. Rohan and Akriti were gobsmacked looking at it. So was Mrs Dave. They had not seen such a wonderful thing before. The timepiece was circular in shape, sky blue in colour and it had four beautiful blue stones studded around the dial. It also had a long tail at the bottom which had two small green leaves as a design. The minute and hour hand were thick black and the seconds hand was thin but golden. The numbers written inside were not so stylish, but had a very different font.

Avni and Rohan both looked a bit puzzled and looked at it from different angles. They liked the timepiece very much so they decided to purchase it. 'I think this is a perfect one. We can buy this. Isn't it, aunt?' asked Rohan, in an exciting tone, grinning wide.

'Yeah fine, whatever you say so,' said Mrs Dave smiling back at him. 'So, we have few colour papers, a pen stand, and a wall clock. Let us go to the billing counter now.' She stuffed the timepiece into the trolley and took the children with her.

They paid the bill at the counter and took the shopping bag and strode out of Cerulean Essence towards their car with umbrellas open as it was raining. They drove back home at around six, too late for tea time so they skipped the tea and milk and instead had some tasty snacks. They brought Tulip back from the neighbour's house but she was still very lazy and went inside her cat house to doze off.

'I like cup-cakes, a lot,' said Avni, stuffing fourth piece of cup-cake in her mouth. 'Yeah, me too,' said Akriti, still eating the first piece. Rohan glanced at her and gave a short laugh as he helped himself with his fourth piece.

'Well, when should we watch the newly released movie- *THE INCONSPICUOUS ASTEROID?* I have heard it from many of my friends, it's just fantastic,' said Akriti in a thrilling voice.

'Umm...yeah, even I heard the same. I think we should watch it in the next week. Till that time mom and dad will also arrive. Aunt, you, and uncle will also come with us,' said Rohan trying to find fifth piece of cup-cake on the table.

'Yes, sure. Gayatri would have come but then, now she has shifted to New York for her studies, she might return only in her vacations,' said Mrs Dave, arranging the kitchen stuff at right place. Gayatri was Mrs Dave's daughter who was pursuing her education from New York.

'It's been a long time, we met Gayatri,' said Avni getting up from her place, as she lost the hope of getting another cup-cake, since the plates were empty.

They helped their aunt in clearing the plates and then went to finish their homework. They were sitting at the common study table. Avni and Rohan were busy with their Science homework and Akriti was doing Social Studies subject. The twins could not concentrate much but Akriti blowed at them so they could do their work properly. She had been very specific with them about studies, all the times.

It was not raining at all and Tulip was sleeping in her comfortable cat house without any disturbance. The trio was still finishing their homework and they had completely forgotten about the new timepiece and other stuff they had purchased from Cerulean Essence.

'What's the time? We didn't have dinner yet…aah…its half past eight, I think aunt might have prepared the dinner,' said Rohan, in a drained-out voice. 'Let's go and sit outside in the drawing room. We will video call mom and dad, till the time aunt gets the things ready.'

They video called their parents and talked to them for twenty minutes. Even their grandparents had a conversation with them. It was full of laughs and jokes. Unfortunately, Mrs Parikh ended the laughing session by reminding them of her anger if they, by any chance troubled Mrs Dave, her sister.

'No, mom we are not troubling her. By the way you can ask her, if you really doubt that,' said Avni frowning.

'Anjali, they are well behaved. Do not worry. They help me in the kitchen work as well…and you know they are my cuties and lovelies,' said Mrs Dave hugging the three together.

'Alright Neha. I obviously believe you…' said Mrs Parikh smiling slightly, comforting her mind that things were right at the other end.

'Mom, do you know, we went for a bit of shopping in Cerulean Essence. We purchased some stationery stuff and a beautiful timepiece,' said Akriti with gleaming eyes, bringing the image of the magnificent clock in front of her eyes.

'I made a new friend in the shop, Robin Spencer who is new to this area,' said Rohan grinning. 'We really….'

The conversation continued a little and later it started raining so much that the rain splashed over the windows which made a loud noise. Nothing could be heard if anyone spoke. The sky grew darker than ever and thunders grew louder. The clouds gathering above made the weather eerie.

After the dinner, the trio and Mrs Dave were binge watching some online shows on the laptop and the weather had turned very chilly so all of them had a warm decoction drink which consisted of different herbal extracts of different plants. They had a nice gala time till half past ten at night, only when Mrs Dave realised that it was a bit late and she asked everyone to go to bed as next day again they had their school. Avni kept thinking about a holiday in school due to incessant rains in Mumbai and even dreamt of getting a holiday and photographing around the house windows of the beautiful rainy weather outside.

But soon after sometime she woke up since another dream disturbed her mind a bit. She saw the timepiece they had brought suddenly speaking something to her and Rohan, but at a different place, rather a different planet and someone kept saying 'World of Time' loudly in her head. Earlier too she had experienced similar dream where someone just kept saying 'World of Time' repeatedly in her head. Her eyes felt heavier than usual and difficult to open wide, she looked at the ceiling above and gave a sigh. 'What sort of connection did she and Rohan possess with that dream?' thought Avni but could not conclude anything. The next moment she was in deep sleep.

Rohan suddenly remembered while he was almost going to doze off, that he had not unpacked the timepiece which he had bought for his room wall. He decided to do the same, on next day after school.

Flummoxed

The next morning was bright and clear. Unfortunately, there were no school group notifications on Avni's only-for-school-purpose mobile phone regarding a holiday in school since the weather was much better and it was not raining at all. She thought that probably it did not rain only because 'rain' did not like to give a holiday from school to students like her who would be more than happy for a day off.

She saw that Akriti was up before her and she was revising Physics formulas. 'We have an objective type practice test today, so I am revising for that, don't disturb me,' said Akriti with a stern expression.

She went to the kitchen to greet her aunt and she found out that Rohan too had woken up before her. He was drinking water, standing in the kitchen. 'Good morning aunt. Hey brother, how come you and Akriti are up before me? Don't we wake up at the same time? I didn't even hear any alarm clock ringing,' said Avni. Mrs Dave smiled at her and nodded, cutting some fruits.

'I guess you were busy dreaming about a day off from school. Taking photographs of the rainy sky from balcony, windows etc...' said Rohan smiling at her. Avni grinned back at him and went inside to get ready for school reluctantly. As usual her twin brother had recognised what was up on her mind which was not surprising for her.

They left on time for school since Mrs Dave ensured that none of them got punishment for coming late. Akriti was busy revising the formulas in her mind while climbing the staircase and went to her class. The twins were discussing about the timepiece they had to unpack when they returned back and reached the class when the final bell rang for students entering in the school.

After the first lecture, before the next teacher arrived, Avni remembered her strange dream she had experienced for the second time. She felt of discussing it with her brother in the lunch break.

But even after they returned from school, she could not tell it to her brother and felt nervous. Rohan realised that his sister is upset about something but he was busy thinking about a school football match while the three of them were having snacks. Mrs Dave grabbed their attention by asking- 'are there any extra-curricular events taking place in your school?'

Rohan replied instantly, 'Yes of course. We have cricket and football matches. I will participate for sure.'

'Yes, and we have elocution competition, poster making activity as well', said Avni forgetting about her dream. She then turned her head to see the time and it struck her that she and her brother had to open the timepiece. 'Excuse me aunt, Rohan and I must unpack the new wall clock which we had purchased from Cerulean Essence. So, shall we do that now? We have almost finished our snacks too,' she said looking at her more than half empty plate of strawberry waffle.

'Yeah sure, why not. Do you need to take permission for that Avni?' replied Mrs Dave sweetly and then she looked at Akriti who was eating her waffle quietly without uttering a word.

'Now Akriti, how much did you score in today's test? I see, that must be the only reason you are sitting so quietly. Maybe, you lost half a mark which has made you upset, isn't it?' asked Mrs Dave, giving a short laugh and patting Akriti on her head.

'No, it was objective type test, so I lost one full mark due to one wrong option which I chose. That is so embarrassing,' said Akriti frowning.

'Aww…' said Rohan giggling to which Akriti gave a very sharp look so he and Avni quickly went inside to open the timepiece immediately before their elder sister would make up her mind to take them forcefully for doing homework.

'I think I kept the box inside my cupboard, right?' said Rohan scratching his head.

'I don't know,' said Avni glancing around here and there.

Rohan took out a large box from the cupboard in which they had brought that beautiful timepiece and kept it on the floor. He and his sister started to unpack the box.

'Wow, that is the best thing I have ever brought for myself. Isn't it Avni?' asked Rohan taking out the timepiece slowly and carefully.

'Yes indeed, Rohan,' replied Avni to him with gleaming eyes and shivering a bit as the weather had suddenly gone cold and wind was blowing heavily. The window pane was moving, making a creaky noise.

She stared at the clock for a minute along with her brother. It was truly magnificent, simply bewitching, Avni felt. Rohan as well. But slowly some strange feeling was getting into their head, they looked disturbed and worrisome; both felt the same. One minute, two minutes still looking at the timepiece. An image was coming in front of their eyes, a person- someone unknown. Not able to recollect. Then a sound came repeatedly – 'World of Time', 'World of Time…'

They went somewhere deep in thoughts and called out each other's name- 'Avni and Rohan.' They felt dazed and puzzled. There was a searing pain in their head which made them feel strangely uncomfortable. 'What was all that about?' they thought, but still lost somewhere, they could not speak, eyes staring at the clock.

'So do you still remember, the things which happened at that time?' said a voice suddenly.

They slowly gathered proper consciousness and glanced around. Whose voice was that?

'Rohan, who spoke just now?' asked Avni in a perplexed tone and her hands went stone cold. 'What were we doing now? I saw something very strange, I do not know, I….'

'Even I saw something, Avni. I am feeling very disturbed. I think I will have a bad headache now,' said Rohan touching his head.

'That is quite obvious,' said that voice again in a very deep tone for a change.

The twins looked here and there, towards the door as well to see if someone was standing there.

'Not at the door, my dears, behind you,' said the same voice, standing at the window side.

The twins turned their heads to see and the pair of eyes stared at the figure standing in front of them. Avni and Rohan stood there in amazement, thinking, what is this happening?

Their mouths were open, eyes still on the figure and minds in bewilderment.

'Robin Spencer?' said Rohan, his heart was pounding and felt nervous.

'How is that possible?' asked Avni who looked at Rohan and into the box they had to open. 'My word, where has the timepiece gone, Rohan?'

The two looked so surprised and could not understand what was exactly happening. They could not even tell in what kind of a state their mind was.

'Oh, do not be confused and surprised, I am the timepiece you brought in. I am Robin Spencer, the Timekeeper of World of Time,' he said in an exaggerated tone.

'What? Timekeeper? You?'

'Yes, of course, my dears. We met at Cerulean Essence first, isn't it? And immediately after that you found me, means the timepiece at the shelf,' he replied.

'You will not believe easily, right? Wait a second,' said Robin smiling.

He waved a dark black pouch at them, which was in his hand. It looked thirty centimetres in length, but he took out a small glass of about ten centimetres from it and then two more things were taken out which were recognisable to the twins.

'Strawberry and Garlic,' said Robin Spencer and squeezed the two things into the glass and a liquid like thing fell from the strawberry and garlic. The mixture boiled on its own in the glass and then he drank it.

He had turned into the timepiece.

Avni and Rohan were flummoxed. For a few minutes they couldn't sink in the reality. They felt as if all this was a dream and nothing else.

But the timepiece just spoke in, 'Still not able to believe? You will surely understand when the whole story gets into your head. You will know the purpose of all this by that time.' The timepiece which was in the box now, could be seen with two hands protruding out, two eyes and a mouth to speak. The hour, minute and seconds hand were clearly visible showing the current time to the twins. Literally a wall clock was speaking to them, unbelievably.

Rohan finally broke his silence and said in a confused tone, 'Can you please explain us then? I....'

Avni interrupted him and said- 'Rohan, do you know I did experience a very strange dream twice till date. Last night only I saw a timepiece saying something to me. I could not see the timepiece; it was inconspicuous but I heard a voice which sounded different although.'

Rohan immediately responded by saying – 'Even I have experienced such kind of dream twice. Exactly like the one which you told, but I don't remember the date and day when I had seen it…'

Robin suddenly said in a very pressing tone, lying inside the box, 'Hmm...I see. You two, now listen to me carefully. Whatever I am going to tell is the truth, nothing is a myth. I am Robin Spencer, Timekeeper of the *World of Time*. I am here from another planet whose name I just mentioned. I live in the *Hill Tower* of the city of *Clockhist*. You two possess a connection with the planet....'

Avni and Rohan exchanged their extremely baffled looks with each other and again turned their heads towards the timepiece to listen further. They were getting ice cold, unbelievably.

The Timekeeper continued, 'Your past birth is associated with the World of Time. Before you were born on Earth, you lived on that planet. I have always known you both as very kind-hearted friends to me and mischievous to the core. Avni, your dream was just because of that. You and Rohan are strongly associated to our planet. As you both have experienced this dream, I must tell that this is your re-birth. I cannot tell you the story hidden behind your re-birth. I am helpless. With a lot of hard work, I have approached you both...'

Avni and Rohan again exchanged the same perplexed look and the pounding in their heart went on increasing than ever. 'Story behind our re-birth?' wondered the twins. They were extremely scared now.

'I had to meet you again, for a paramount purpose. We three have to come together to defeat someone. Someone who is extremely cruel, who has no respect for time and just hungry for power. I need your help. I had a vision few months ago that at a certain point of time, I have to go searching for my friends Avni and Rohan to fight the evil,' said Robin closing his small pair of eyes which looked strangely funny.

Rohan was gobsmacked to listen to this so he hesitantly asked in a very low tone, 'Where is this planet? How can we believe you? If you may provide some proof about all the stuff you said just now...'

'Proof? My presence itself is a proof, isn't that enough dear Rohan? But still I can show you something,' said Robin Spencer in a slightly cheerful tone and he took the same pouch in his hands and opened it again to take out something.

Avni and Rohan looked extremely curious and wanted to see the proof immediately. Robin took out two very small photos of the size of an eraser and a magnifying glass of the same size and handed it to Rohan.

Rohan raised his eyebrows and said mockingly- 'I think this is too big. You should have provided some proof even smaller than this.'

Avni didn't laugh at this rather she looked very tense and took the photos and magnifying glass from Rohan. She focussed the magnifying glass on both photos one by one. The first photo contained a large tower on which Robin Spencer was hanging as a timepiece and below that, three people were standing. Two of them were the twins themselves. The third person was another girl and she was smiling widely. But Avni and Rohan did not bother to ask about her at present.

The next photo also contained the same people but a different place and Robin was in human form with one person extra this time who was a man possessing a grave expression on his face. Again, the twins did not bother to ask about the extra person.

'Alright, the magnifying glass was of little help. So, these photos indicate our presence on that planet,' said Avni nodding her head. Rohan did not say anything this time and wondered about what this planet was exactly.

Robin took back the photos and continued to speak, 'Our planet is not situated in space, by the way. It is somewhere on Earth, may be between the air particles but is invisible of course…we can travel to and from it by a special object…'

Avni and Rohan heard everything carefully but Avni was desperate to ask a question- 'We were born on Earth and earlier you mentioned that we were descendants of the World of Time. We want to know the story of our birth…'

Robin shook his head in the box and the entire wall clock which was visible to the twins moved from left to right and vice-versa. 'At the right time I will tell you both, but for now please do not ask this question.'

Avni and Rohan were becoming desperate to know, so they tried to sneak out the information regarding their re-birth many a times but in vain. So, they gave up and asked something else-

'You were telling that we need to defeat someone who is extremely cruel and…,' said Avni leaving her sentence incomplete and looked hopefully at Robin.

The Timekeeper again took the pouch, this time he took out only garlic from it, squeezed it into the small glass and again a liquid like thing came out from the garlic. It boiled on its own again. He drank it saying, 'It tastes horrible,' and he revived back into his human form.

He sat on the floor in front of the twins and spoke in a grave tone, 'That's truly an important question, Avni. The person whom you are asking about is a mysterious one. But he is not at all good. He just yearns for power. This time he has crossed his limits and is going to add the twenty fifth hour of time to all the clocks on our planet, which is against the rule of nature, since we have twenty-four hours as a day's limit. Exactly like planet Earth. No one knows how he is going to achieve that, but yes, we have people to investigate regarding his whereabouts and stuff. The name of the evil person is Capvile.'

Robin rolled his eyes from Rohan to Avni and looked at their expressions after completing his sentence.

The twins gaped at him in utter bewilderment.

Robin continued ahead, 'I need your help for defeating his ambitions. I could have done it alone but I preferred taking my best friends for this mission, of course you two do not remember about your past birth and all except for the strange dreams you experienced but, I haven't forgotten you.'

Avni was gradually sinking in the facts. She then spoke, 'Robin, we trust you of course for all these incidences happened back-to-back with us, they might be carrying a reason and I am slowly understanding about it. We will help you…' and then she looked at Rohan who was sitting beside her with pursed lips and his eyes revealed that he agreed with his sister.

'I am thankful,' said Robin with a wide grin and satisfaction.

Rohan opened his mouth looking outside the window staring at the rain, 'What about our parents? What should we tell them?' and then he looked at Robin, continuing his sentence, 'Do you want us to say, hey mom and dad we have been invited to another planet by our dear friend Robin, should we go?'

Robin gave a short laugh and replied, 'Do you really think I don't have an answer for that. Of course, I have. I planned about all this, before coming here.'

'What do you mean by I planned?' asked Avni questioningly.

Robin just smiled and took his pouch in front.

'I will make a decoction out of a special plant's leaves mixed with almond powder as you have seen me doing with other ingredients before. You will have to drink that decoction and you will be divided into two forms of yourself. One pair of yours will stay at home and the other pair has to come with me,' said Robin.

The twins stared at him with widened eyes.

'You call that decoction? We will drink it? Two forms?' said Rohan breathing heavily out of stress.

'I do not understand all this,' said Avni as the pounding in her heart started to increase again.

'If you do that, you will not have to answer your parents. For your kind information preparing decoctions and using them is the way to get many things done on our planet,' said Robin with a sweet smile.

'But won't it be an indirect lie? We never lie to our parents, for your kind information,' said Rohan in a slightly furious tone.

'It is not a lie my dear friend Rohan,' replied Robin shaking his head in disagreement. 'What I think is, we are heading for a good purpose and taking a risk like this will help us a lot.'

'Yes, you should never lie to anyone, but Rohan, try to change your perspective in this case,' continued Robin coming out of the box, now in the air.

Avni and Rohan looked at each other.

Robin continued again, 'Listen Avni and Rohan. You might have heard from your parents and others too that time waits for none. It comes and it flies. I am not forcing you, after all the choice lies with you. You must choose. But being a Timekeeper, I advise you not to waste time and try to take a decision. Of course, I had expected my best friends to support me who do not remember their dear friend Robin from their past birth.'

Avni and Rohan pondered for a while about how difficult all this was and what could be the right decision.

Few minutes passed and Avni spoke in a grave tone, 'I am ready to help, Robin.'

Rohan seemed extremely serious for the first time in his life and said- 'See Robin, all this is happening in quick succession. Suddenly how will you feel if someone asks you to take a decision like this? It is difficult, even more difficult than our test papers. But frankly I must tell, my heart is telling me somewhere to help you out and I always listen to my heart. Yes, I will also help.'

Robin smiled again and closed his eyes feeling satisfied.

'Well, aren't you both interested to know about how are we travelling to the planet, considering the fact that its invisible?' asked Robin cheerfully.

'Oh yes, of course. Tell us, how are we supposed to travel and what all things we need to carry,' said Avni.

'Most importantly, when are we supposed to leave?' asked Rohan folding his hands as he shivered a bit, since the weather was getting colder.

'We are leaving right now, that too using a TTSM short for Time Travelling Speedo Machine,' said Robin excitedly. 'But before that, you need to intake the decoction made out of the special plant leaves and almond powder.'

'Yeah, we will do that, but what is this TSM?' asked Avni getting up from her place.

'You missed one T, it is TTSM. Do not make a mistake Avni. Time Travelling Speedo Machine will take us to the World of Time. It is quite big but will fit in here,' said Robin looking around everywhere nodding his head.

'I want to see your TTS right now. Please show it fast,' said Rohan, looking slightly excited.

'Oh, dear Rohan, you missed the M. It is TTSM. Do not make a mistake Rohan,' said Robin and he took out a piece of paper from his pouch which contained some image.

Avni and Rohan were quite impressed with the fascinating pouch and wanted to ask Robin about how did it carry so many things but they gave up the thought as Robin started to explain them something.

'Look at this image. It is the TTSM I was talking about. I will pour a decoction containing Peachpuff and Cadet Blue extract on this image and within seconds our TTSM will be here,' said Robin and put the image back into the pouch.

'And before that you want us to drink that decoction of yours first which will divide us into two,' said Rohan and then Avni spoke after him suddenly, 'We are ready.' Rohan stared at her.

Avni and Rohan closed their eyes and took the decoction from the two small glasses which Robin provided them. It tasted horrible. It went down their throats. Both felt very strange. They did not open their eyes until Robin asked them to.

'You may open your eyes,' uttered Robin in a soft voice.

The twins opened their eyes and saw the other pair of themselves standing beside them, smiling. The other pair of twins smiled at them and said nothing. Avni and Rohan felt as if a mirror was kept in front of them and they were looking at their reflection.

'Remember, since they are a part of you, they will feel what you feel and what they feel will be felt by you, but this will happen when you think of each other,' said Robin without a pause. 'They will study exactly how you do, there is no difference except that you will be on separate missions.'

Avni and Rohan asked the other pair of twins a few questions and they expected exactly the same thing which the other pair answered. The five people in the room were standing still for few seconds and they heard meowing of the cat Tulip outside the closed door. Avni and Rohan suspected that either their aunt Mrs Dave or Akriti might be there along with the cat. So, they quickly sent the other pair of twins outside hiding themselves and Robin behind the room cupboard and they were right. Akriti was standing outside with Tulip and asked, 'Does it take so much time to assemble a clock on the wall?'

'We have not put it up yet, we were busy admiring it. Let us go and play Akriti,' said Avni, the divided part of the original one.

After everything was settled, Robin, Rohan and Avni felt a deep satisfaction. Now they were finally ready to go.

Robin poured the decoction containing Peachpuff and Cadet Blue extract on the image which he showed before. After that, the piece of paper whirled in the air with a lot of speed and a green light flashed out of it which made Avni and Rohan close their eyes but Robin just kept smiling.

They felt the light fading slowly and as they opened their eyes, both jumped to their feet. They went goggle-eyed. The Time Travelling Speedo Machine (TTSM), was in front of them. It was pure white in colour and large but could easily fit inside the room. It had two big glass windows in circular shape and an automatic entrance door which was entirely opaque and silver in colour. As they went inside, their eyes looked utterly astonished. Robin was just observing their expressions.

There was a switchboard inside which Robin explained, was for the lights and pure air inside the machine. The twins saw a large black button on a bonnet kind of a thing and Robin explained it was the front part of the TTSM. The button was meant for the start of the machine, after which within a few seconds the TTSM turns invisible in the air. So, Robin explained them in short, 'It is the start and disappear button.'

'It is truly amazing. I think we have correctly made a decision,' said Rohan with satisfaction.

Avni was still in awe and could not utter anything, so she kept turning her head around everywhere to take a glimpse of the interior part of the Time Travelling Speedo Machine.

'Now it's the time to begin a new journey my friends. Within a few seconds I will press the black button and then off we go,' said Robin Spencer, looking at the special black button.

Avni and Rohan were ready to serve a special purpose which was meant for the good of the people of the World of Time. They were unaware of the planet, unaware of difficulties lying ahead, unaware of how they were going to stay apart from their lovable family and house. Many questions still troubled them, but they had made a choice on their own. It was their decision and now there was no point in reverting back. They chose to go with the flow.

'So, are we ready friends?' asked Robin, approaching the black button which he considered now as a symbol of a new beginning and journey.

'Take these headphones. You need to wear them as it helps you in standing still. There is no chance of feeling uneasy while travelling if you are wearing them. I requested a scientist to invent them and he did. Perfect they are,' said Robin offering them pairs of blue coloured headphones which were kept beside the black button.

They did as Robin instructed them. He too put up the headphones and pressed the black button. The TTSM whirled in the air and went round and round for five times and then it disappeared. Since the headphones were on, the three enjoyed the experience. Avni and Rohan felt they were in a car and as they looked outside the window, only darkness was visible and nothing else.

Within a few seconds, they were about to enter a different planet...

World of Time

The automatic countdown in the machine began which Avni, Rohan and Robin could hear faintly due to the headphones. Five…four…three…two…one.

The TTSM started to lower down slowly and Avni tried to look outside the window if she could see anything on the new planet but in vain. It was still dark outside. She scowled slightly and was willing to ask Robin about the purpose of the two circular windows since only darkness was visible and nothing else. Meanwhile Rohan was pondering over something hard but no one asked him what he was thinking. He too did not bother to discuss whatever he was pondering about. Robin, the Timekeeper of the planet seemed quite excited as he had invited his friends to his world. He also remembered the significant mission which was the main reason for all that had happened in the past few hours.

TTSM finally lowered onto the ground and it stopped. The destination had arrived.

'Rohan and Avni, you may remove the headphones as we have reached the World of Time,' said Robin Spencer with a wide grin on his face. He looked extremely happy.

Avni and Rohan felt anxious. They slowly removed the headphones and the trio approached the opaque automatic door which slid open. The twins stepped out with Robin.

They had entered the backyard of a humongous building in front. The backyard consisted of beautiful green grass and large bushes and trees. Avni and Rohan looked around in amazement.

'Welcome to the World of Time,' said Robin aloud with his hands stretched out. Rohan looked at him and gave a short laugh. 'That is a different style of yours, Robin, to welcome us,' he said nodding his head.

'This place is beautiful, Robin. By the way, which place is this? Which building is this?' asked Avni looking at the tall building which had glass window panes at the backside.

'This is the city of *Clockhist*. My birthplace of course. Well, when I opened my eyes for the first time, surprisingly I found myself hanging as a timepiece on the Hill Tower,' said Robin widening his eyes as he recollected the day when he was born. 'This building is named as *Victorious Aura*. We are now going to meet a special person here. You would be more than happy to meet the person,' said Robin in continuation. Rohan wondered who they were going to meet but did not ask anything.

The weather around was not very cold, but the sky looked extremely clear. The twins along with Robin headed towards the front part of the building and it was equally beautiful as the backside. On the right and left near the entrance of the building there were small green bushes lined up alluringly. A large green space on both sides beyond the bushes was icing on the cake. There was an automatic security system before entering the building which beeped if any metallic object was detected. The security man standing beside was staring at the trio as if he had seen some different species on the planet. 'Do we look different?' asked Robin in a slightly annoyed tone and they headed inside.

Avni moved her eyes everywhere in the hall-like area and saw a white board on which, 'Reception area' was written in bold blue letters. Rohan was thinking that everything was exactly similar to their planet except the fact that there was no Timekeeper who could speak and transform into human using decoctions. So, he found everything quite normal, but he was unaware of the things that were going to happen further.

Robin said in a soft and low tone- 'maintain silence as much as you can and follow me to the reception counter.'

There were very few people in that area. A lady was sitting with a coffee mug on a large pink sofa kept exactly on the opposite side of the counter and a man was standing near the newspaper stand with a newspaper open. His face was not visible at all and he did not move an inch either. Apart from them a staff member was cleaning the floor and looked up at the three new entries only once and then got busy with his work.

They moved near the reception counter. The reception lady smiled at them and wished them, 'good evening' and the pile of papers she was carrying in her hand fell on the floor. Suddenly Avni remembered that she had forgotten about the time going right then. She did not know what was the time and wondered whom she should ask. Then she clapped her head with her hand and spoke to herself saying- 'we have a Timekeeper here and why should I ask anyone else?'

Before she could ask Robin, the reception girl had collected the papers properly and murmured looking for something on the desk, 'Sorry, actually I have a lot of work…I am a bit stressed…messing things up…'

After few seconds the reception lady asked, 'How may I help you?' and straightened her spectacles. She was tall and brown haired. Avni did not like her at all as she seemed a bit poker faced.

'We want to meet the senior most journalist, Mr Ajay Chauhan,' said Robin in firm tone and as he said these words, the twins looked at him and thought simultaneously that this was the person whom they were about to meet.

The lady looked at them in surprise and asked 'You three kids want to meet Mr Ajay Chauhan? The senior most journalist? Sorry but this is not possible without an appointment.'

Rohan gave a short laugh and wondered in mind that- 'does anyone know Robin Spencer, the Timekeeper at all? Or is he just hanging there on the Hill Tower, showing the time to the passers-by on road?'

But the next moment he was left in awe by what Robin did. Avni too looked utterly amazed.

Robin rubbed his palms against each other and showed the left palm to the reception. It was carrying a small symbol of a timepiece which was black in colour. It showed the time as well. The hour hand, minute and second's hand were visible. The second's hand was moving round over the small clock on his palm. It was showing half past four in the clock. Avni and Rohan realised that the time differed by few hours from their city but they were quite dumbfounded at what Robin had showed just now.

The reception girl widened her eyes and opened her mouth slightly and she spoke in a trembling voice, 'R-robin S-spencer, the Timekeeper? I-I am s-sorry sir but I had n-not seen you before in this form. Many a times I have been to the Hill Tower Road but you used to be hanging over there, sir.'

'Yeah, it is quite rare for me to transform into a human, you know, but you might be knowing we use decoctions for such a purpose. Anyways, can we meet Mr Ajay now?' said Robin.

'Yes sir, of course. You need to go on fourth floor. Well, sir, I must tell you for your information that I respect time a lot. I never misuse time,' said the tall lady shaking her head, pretending to be very respectful for time.

'I can very well make out, who uses time correctly and who doesn't,' said Robin with his usual smile. 'Thanks, by the way, for permitting us.'

Avni and Rohan followed Robin towards the staircase instead of lift so Avni asked him, 'Why aren't we taking the lift?'

'Staircase exercise is pretty good for health, Avni. Avoid using the lift whenever you can,' answered Robin climbing as fast as he could.

The twins said nothing but they remembered about the small replica of timepiece showed by Robin on his palm. They thought simultaneously as they did many a times, to not to ask anything right now but surely, they would when the right time had approached.

The twins did not get tired climbing the staircase as they were quite used to it. Neither Robin was tired. After three minutes, they finally reached the fourth floor. The passageway was huge. There were several large cabins on the right, left and front with glass doors and a common thing written on them in stylish font- VA.

'I suppose VA means Victorious Aura, isn't it Robin?' said Avni who looked quite impressed seeing the large cabins.

'Yes, you are right,' replied Robin showing a thumbs up to her.

'Robin, which cabin belongs to, er-Mr Ajay?' asked Rohan moving his eyes off all the cabins. 'And most importantly why are we here?'

'I know Rohan you might be having loads of questions and I am sure you will receive the answer for each one of them. Do not worry, you will get to know the reason behind meeting Mr Ajay. By the way the last cabin in front is the one,' said Robin pointing out at last cabin.

Avni was quite excited to meet a journalist and at the same time she felt a pounding in her stomach out of nervousness as she took every step towards the cabin. They stood in front of the glass door and as Robin tried to open it, the handle made a noise and he took his hand off with a sudden jerk as the handle carried an electric current.

'Oh no! The reception lady did not tell me that Mr Ajay has put up decoction on his door for security reasons that is why I am unable to open it with handle,' said Robin shaking his hand as he felt a burning sensation. 'How should we go inside?'

Avni and Rohan wanted to ask about the decoction concept as well, how does it work and all but now the question was how to go inside. Before Robin could do anything, a security guard approached them from behind. The twins looked a bit afraid as he was very tall and carried a large stick in his hand along with a register book like thing.

Robin showed him his left palm as he did at the reception counter. The small timepiece was visible and Avni bent her head forward to have a look at it once again as that was the thing which fascinated her the most.

'Alright, so the Timekeeper wants to go inside Mr Ajay's cabin. Wait a minute sir, I have a list of decoctions put up at certain cabins for security reasons. I will tell you the correct one for cabin number seven,' said the security guard in a soft toned voice. Rohan was surprised after listening to his polite tone since it didn't suit his thug like personality.

'Sir, do you have grey and orange cement in your decoction provider pouch? That is the required thing,' said the guard in such a low voice which could be heard only by the trio.

'Oh my god! What sort of decoction is this?' asked Rohan in utmost bewildered tone. Avni looked horrified and astonished both.

Robin was nodding his head and spoke in a low tone- 'yes, it is extracted from cement plant and I have it. Thank you, Mr…'

'You can call me Mr Tiger as others do,' said the security guard with a smile. 'I told the decoction ingredients of security only to you sir, as you are the Timekeeper. Otherwise, I have to do it every time.'

'Alright Mr Tiger, thank you very much,' said Robin as the guard turned back to go. He took out his black pouch. He put grey and orange cement powder in the small glass and the mixture boiled on its own turning chocolate brown at end. Meanwhile Avni and Rohan were whispering to each other saying, 'Cement plant? I haven't heard of such a thing. I thought that on this planet things were similar to ours but this decoction and all is just getting past my head...'

'Yeah, you are absolutely right...'

'If you both are done with your discussion, should I pour this decoction?' asked Robin looking at the twins.

'Sure.'

Robin poured the glass ingredients right in front of the cabin door and as he did so, the chocolate brown liquid spilled on the floor disappeared with a blink. The glass door flung open on its own. The trio stepped inside finally. The cabin looked as normal as any office cabin except the walls which carried the pictures of newspapers and journalists. There was a large work desk and chairs around it. A man was sitting on a leather chair, writing something on a page. He was wearing a dark blue coat and a round black hat on his head. He was so busy writing that he could not feel the presence of the trio in his cabin.

Robin wore his usual smile again and spoke, 'Good evening, Mr Ajay. May we come in? I am surprised that you were not alert enough when we entered as you usually are for security reasons.'

The man looked up but did not smile back at all rather he carried a grave expression on his face. 'Of course, I can recognise from the footsteps itself if someone untrustworthy has entered my cabin,' said the man in a very bristly manner.

Robin smiled. The twins were in awe after listening to his statement. He was wearing square shaped spectacles and the twins observed that he was not at all young. His hair was half grey and he had baggy eyes with wrinkles under them. But the man looked confident and his eyes reflected a different intelligence which he possessed.

'Good evening, Robin Spencer,' said Mr Ajay in an earnest tone and looked at the twins standing beside Robin. 'Even if the guard pours the decoction for an untrustworthy person who has impersonated someone, I can very well make out from the footsteps of the person.'

'I didn't know this talent of yours, sir,' replied Robin shrugging his shoulder.

'Take the seat, Robin. Glad to meet you,' said the journalist with a very faint smile. 'Thank you, sir,' said Robin and he sat on the chair offered to him but the twins preferred to stand.

Rohan and Avni glanced at the work desk which looked very clean. Few books were piled up at one side and some blank pages were kept neatly under a paper weight. There was a fascinating pen stand which was a small alarm clock as well. There was a laptop kept on the right side of Mr Ajay's table and Avni tried to bend a little to know the brand name written in black letters on the laptop but Rohan pulled her off whispering- 'check it later, Avni.'

'So, you have brought your friends as you had said Robin Spencer. That's good. You are a man of word by the way…er…sorry you are a clock of word,' said Mr Ajay finding some book in the pile kept on the desk.

'Yes sir. But they do not remember anything from their previous birth on this planet except the fact that one of them dreamt about it', said Robin and suddenly he remembered about introducing the twins and Mr Ajay to each other. 'Ah, I forgot to introduce them. This is Avni Parikh and Rohan Parikh,' he said pointing at them.

'Hello sir. Good evening,' said the twins simultaneously to which Mr Ajay nodded, this time with a slightly bigger smile.

'Rohan and Avni, this is Mr Ajay Chauhan, the senior most journalist of Clockhist city. He works for *Clockhist Enigma* newspaper. Quite famous all over this planet. He has won many accolades in his field and awarded with the best journalist, inspiring leader, and most popular article trophies. These are just a few to name,' said Robin with a pride visible on his face.

'I think that is enough to mention now, Robin Spencer. Should we talk about the main motive for which we have gathered?' asked Mr Ajay with a stern expression. The twins became alert as they were not going to miss on a single word from this paramount discussion because that was the reason they had travelled from Earth to the World of Time, to know exactly what was happening and what they had to do. They stood still with folded hands. Both were anxious at the same time.

'I think Rohan and Avni must be knowing at least a bit of the whole story,' continued Mr Ajay in a low tone, 'about Capvile and his wrong ambitions. I do not know how is he going to add the twenty-fifth hour to the time. That is difficult. But it is surely going to be a trouble for you Robin. It will harm you. The pain of carrying another hour which is artificial is going to be a challenge for you.'

Avni and Rohan looked at Robin who was staring at the desk, the moment Mr Ajay mentioned all this, probably he felt upset they thought.

Robin lifted his eyes up from the desk, saying- 'If the alchemist, Capvile succeeds in his experiment, it will affect the entire World of Time. One of the worst things which is most likely to happen is that the sky will change its colours frequently. It will in turn affect all the water bodies present on this planet. The nature won't tolerate the artificial blunders invented by humans and the consequences are far worse than imagined.'

These facts startled the twins even more.

'But sir, Tara is investigating secretly right, about Capvile?' asked Robin after few seconds raising his eyebrows. The twins wondered who on this planet was Tara. So Avni dared to interrupt in between this discussion and said, 'May I ask who she is?'

'Miss Tara is Mr Ajay's daughter and a to-be-certified-detective at the Clockhist Enigma. She is excellent in her job. She is trying to collect certain clues along with her Informer Spy which will help us to know Capvile's plan,' said Robin in one go to which Mr Ajay nodded in agreement.

Mr Ajay leaned forward on his desk and said, 'Yes, Robin Spencer. They are doing their work, but it is not that easy. Don't you think Capvile will try his best to keep his plans secret? He has done that before too. So many times, he has escaped even after inventing some stupid things which could cause harm to people, why? He used to manipulate every situation leaving no proof against himself. I am pretty sure he will make it look as difficult as he can this time too. He might have even found out that Tara and Informer Spy are behind him.'

'Hmm...I agree with you sir,' replied Robin.

'But the police force also might be searching for him, for stopping the blunder which Capvile is planning for,' said Rohan questioningly.

'See, Rohan, this news has neither been published anywhere in newspapers, nor anyone else apart from a few of us is aware of this. We won't let it out. The main aim of Capvile is to succeed in this task secretly and then publicise it to earn fame and power. Once it is achieved by him nobody can do anything. So, our main aim is to finish his ambitions before he does this blunder,' said Mr Ajay in a soft tone. 'We don't know how did he come to know about the twenty-fifth hour and all. This shows what kind of terrible person he is.'

'Sir, how did you all come to know about this?' asked Avni gathering some courage to interrupt again.

'It is the job of the detectives, Miss Avni, to knock down such secrets from its roots,' said Mr Ajay.

'Mr Ajay, when can we meet Tara? If she has collected some clues, we can help her out,' said Robin hoping for an answer from Mr Ajay.

'I think you will be able to meet her tomorrow. She is not in the city right now, mostly she will return early in the morning tomorrow,' said Mr Ajay straightening his square shaped spectacles. 'Till it gets dark you can show this beautiful city of Clockhist to your friends. Its only fifteen minutes past five.' And suddenly he realised that he was telling the time to the Timekeeper himself for which everyone gave a short laugh.

Robin, Rohan and Avni thanked Mr Ajay for carrying out the discussion regarding Capvile and his plans. They went down the staircase and out of the main entrance gate. Avni and Rohan had started to understand much of the things now. They felt more comfortable, but still all their anxiety was not over. They stopped midway outside the entrance gate and so did Robin.

For almost a minute no one spoke but then Rohan initiated the conversation by saying, 'Robin, we have started to understand things a bit. It was nice meeting Mr Ajay, at least we found out five percent of the information regarding the reason for which we have come here. But this does not solve all our questions.'

'Robin, you had said that our past birth is associated with this planet. But we do not remember about the places, people, and stuff, I just know about the dream I had. Everything else is new for us,' said Avni in one go and gave a deep sigh. She then continued saying- 'definitely it will take time for us to sink in the facts but we'll try our best to help you out.'

'Thanks, Avni. But you know, time is everything. In the morning you both were not aware of what all is coming ahead, then in the afternoon you were in utter amazement…listening to my story and now you both are here. See not a day's difference and your life changed completely. You both chose to go with the flow and accepted the situation wisely. I agree that it will take time for you to know the stuff in here but will understand that better every moment, I suppose,' said Robin staring longingly at a distant green tree.

Avni and Rohan did not say anything but smiled faintly at whatever Robin said.

'By the way, the sun sets at around fifteen minutes past seven here and we have ample of time to explore certain places,' said Robin suddenly remembering about the places which he wanted to show them in the city of Clockhist. 'First we will go to a special store which is beyond your imagination and you will dearly like it, once you are inside that store.'

'What kind of store?' asked Rohan as they started moving ahead and walked past the green bushes on either side. 'And how are we supposed to go there?'

'You will come to know once we reach. We will walk as it is quite near to this Victorious Aura building. Only a few metres and we will be there,' said Robin marching ahead.

Avni listened to Robin a bit absent-mindedly as she remembered something. She could not see the laptop brand when they had been to cabin of Mr Ajay. She felt cross and Rohan realised that at once.

He spoke in a slightly annoyed tone- 'Avni do you really think being concerned about the laptop brand is more important right now?'

Robin kept laughing at this for few seconds.

They moved out of the huge iron gate of the building and walked on the edge of the main road. The sky was partly cloudy but the air was fresh. Many cars went past them in speed but everything looked normal to the twins. They had seen such speeding cars of course. They wondered which store Robin was taking them to. On their left side were beautifully decorated shops which looked neat and clean. A small group of people were arguing in loud voice with the shopkeeper of a clothing shop so Avni thought that probably they had received some defective material and were asking for exchange. Another shop they saw was completely empty. The shopkeeper was standing outside, looking hopeful for some customers to enter.

Robin kept muttering something regarding the World of Time and its people. 'People here are very similar to the ones on Earth. But they are pretty little things which make our planet different from Earth. Like the decoction, you know…and the store which we are going to will surprise you again…'

'Robin, we also want to know this decoction concept in detail. Can you please tell us?' said Avni dragging her feet heavily as she felt a bit drained out now.

'Yeah, I will, when I am free,' said Robin nodding his head. The twins turned their heads towards Robin and thought 'what new surprise will we receive?' and a light cool breeze went past them which felt comforting. The sky looked cloudy but the breeze was soothing.

But there seemed to be no end to shops lined up on the left. They walked over for nearly ten minutes and finally Robin slowed his speed and so the twins. They had stopped in front of the Timekeeper's Store.

A large scarlet board had the letters written in bold blue colour, *Timekeeper's Store.*

But the structure of the store wasn't normal. Avni and Rohan had received another shock in just few hours of time. Again, their mouths were wide open and eyes stunned. The store was in the shape of a humongous circular clock with the base of two legs. The circular border of clock was scarlet red and on the front portion it showed numbers from one to twelve with three black hands (hour, minute and seconds). One more startling thing was that it displayed the present time exactly like what was there on the left palm of Robin Spencer.

'That's bizarre!' said Avni with goggle-eyed expressions.

'That's extraordinary!' said Rohan looking jolted. 'But how couldn't we see such a huge thing when we were approaching here? We could see it only when we came in front of it.'

'It is because of the decoction they have used. Probably a mixture of coal and steel balls...not sure...' said Robin thinking hard.

With the same expressions the twins turned their heads and looked at Robin and thought- 'What? Coal and steel balls?'

'Things aren't exactly the same here as on our planet,' said Rohan staring at the front portion of the store where the large numbers were written. 'As soon as I start thinking that this world is similar to ours, the next moment I come across such things which I couldn't have even dreamt of.'

'Well, one thing I wanted to tell is that the store opens only between ten to twelve in morning and it admits the people at that time for them to tour inside. Many people who came in the morning must be still there in the store. The exit door is on the back side of this huge store and a ticket is required to enter,' said Robin lucidly.

'Then how can we go inside? We do not have any tickets and why did you bring us here then?' asked Avni sadly as she thought they would not be allowed in.

'I am the Timekeeper. I do not require a ticket to enter the store and so don't you both, as you will be coming with me,' said Robin sternly. 'I am turning back to my original clock manifestation for that.'

He took out the decoction pouch from his pocket and squeezed strawberry and garlic in the mini glass to gain his original form. He hung in the air with two hands, a pair of eyes and a mouth. They walked over and stood very close to the Timekeeper store. The twins could not see any entrance gate to go inside and before they could ask Robin, he said quickly- 'Hello, this is Robin Spencer, the one and only Timekeeper. Can you please let me in?'

A very clear and lucid voice (a lady's voice) could be heard from somewhere so the twins stared at the huge structure searching for something like a speaker. But nothing could be seen so they just heard what the voice said- 'Hello sir. Welcome to Timekeeper's store. It would be our pleasure to let you in. But please confirm whether the two people standing with you are your guests or some intruders.'

'We are not intruders!' exclaimed Rohan displeasingly. Avni too scowled at this.

'Sorry guys,' whispered Robin hanging in the air and then spoke loudly replying back to the lady- 'They are my friends. Please allow them as well.'

'Okay. Thank you for confirming, sir. You need to move thirty steps back from the position where you are standing so that we can open the gateway of our store,' said the voice. 'For your information I must tell that the store gateway opens up in front. So please do the needful.'

The twins obeyed at once without asking anything since that would just take more time for Robin explaining everything from scratch. They were excited to explore the store along with Robin so they just followed whatever they had been asked to.

As they moved backward, Avni teased Robin by saying- 'you can't walk right now so keep flying backwards!'

Rohan was counting the steps properly so it was easy for Robin to move backwards. All three stood still thirty steps behind. Suddenly a loud hooting sound came which went past their ears and made them jump at once. Robin just smiled. Avni was staring at the scarlet red front portion of the store. But a few seconds later the twins realised that their eyes were moving down and it was not long before they saw that the scarlet red portion fell with a thud on the floor. The large timepiece's hands and numbers visible earlier were pressed against the ground as the entrance opened in the front.

'So, this is the entrance,' said Rohan and they dragged their feet anxiously and walked ahead. Robin went through the air, no doubt. There was an empty hall beyond such a large store. Only two guards were seen pacing down the entire hall, probably they did not realise that the entrance had just opened because around this time normally the entrance would not open unless it was Robin who wanted to enter inside at whatever time suited him. They were busy talking to each other pacing from one corner to the other.

The interior of the *Timekeeper's Store* was perfectly normal unlike the outer circular portion. It was like any other normal store. 'If you have inspected the store with your eyes, can we step in?' said Robin jokingly as he made them realise that they had to go in.

The trio went past the entrance which was the outer circular portion of the store earlier. It had now turned into a slope on which they went walking.

Exploring more

'Good evening, sir. What a pleasant surprise,' said one of the guards as both of them stopped pacing realising that Robin Spencer had entered the store. 'I suppose you have come with your guests today.'

'Good evening. Of course, I have come with my guests,' said Robin to the guard.

The store entrance had walls decorated with Robin's photos with several people whom the twins surely were not aware of. Also, there were paintings consisting of Robin hanging on the Hill Tower (his birth place) and people standing below it with smiling faces. There was a large counter on the left and dark brown couch on the right. At the other end of the hall, there was an elevator which led downwards and not upwards, which surprised the twins.

'We need the entry bands, please,' said Robin after a pause of few seconds.

'Sir, you do not need them. Your guests need to wear them although,' said the other guard who took out a few bands from a glass box kept on the counter. 'Select any two, dear children.'

Rohan and Avni glanced at each other and selected one grey and one blue band. Each band had a quote written by Robin himself. Before Avni opened her mouth to read, Robin spoke aloud without reading it- 'The grey band in your hand says- '*The definition of past, present, and future comes from time. The time that was, the time that is and the time that will be*'

The blue band in Rohan's hand had the quote which Robin read aloud- '*Great ideas can be mapped out in the present instead of wasting time and regretting later*'

'That is simply awesome, Robin. You should write a book consisting of all your motivating quotes compiled together nicely,' said Avni as she suddenly felt very influenced by Robin's quotes on time.

'I have written a book already-*Exclusive Compilation of Great Thoughts by Timekeeper*', said Robin with a huge smile.

Rohan did not listen to the title of the book which Robin told as something else intrigued him. The elevator going downwards. The *Timekeeper's Store* had a unique structure and the entire store was built underground and was enormous in size as well. 'Come on Robin, I want to go down,' said Rohan approaching the elevator.

They reached the elevator end. Rohan and Avni felt as if they were some tourists on a long tour, exploring an interesting place. Robin behaved as the guide elucidating them every object and every place in detail. 'There are ten sub-outlets inside my store. Every sub-outlet is known as a cottage. Let us visit the first cottage here on the left,' he said while pointing out at the large cottage which looked extremely fascinating and grand.

There were five to six people in the cottage helping themselves with a few purchases and as they saw Robin flying in the air in his timepiece manifestation, they wished him immediately- 'Hello sir' and bowed in front of him. Rohan and Avni were amazed at the respect people gave to Robin, the Timekeeper. Robin had to greet back too with a smile and he knew that everyone will be wishing him until he leaves the store.

Avni gave a short laugh and said- 'funny people' after looking at short man's strange combination of pink and yellow, but she spoke in low tone so that no one could hear, but Rohan had heard it and he giggled along with his sister.

As they headed a bit, few more people gathered and wished Robin.

'Hello everyone, now if you all could please allow me to guide my guests…' he said and the trio made their way through the small crowd.

'Robin, I want to know about these clocks, they are so different,' said Rohan who seemed to be quite curious.

'Yeah, not only different, they are fantastic and fascinating,' said Avni picking one rectangular, neon-green timepiece from the clock full shelf, it had no design but a string on its neon green border, a rose gold string.

'As it contains this rose gold string, it is a Rose Essence clock. This string is made from rose plant and embedded into it. It is fully natural,' said Robin lowering down in the air and touching the timepiece with his short fingers. 'String made from rose plant?' asked the twins simultaneously.

'Well Robin, the plants and trees on this planet seem very interesting to me,' said Rohan with a sigh.

'Yes, we will see them when we get time,' replied Robin.

'Do you mean when we get you, right? Said Avni and laughed hard. When we get time, doesn't fit!'

'Avni, that wasn't much funny,' said Robin taking out another timepiece, which was shaped like dragon. It was purple in colour and had pointed wings like dragon and a long tail at the bottom of it. The numbers inside were also pointed and sharp.

The three hands were black and still, as it had no battery.

'My word, I cannot believe if something like this would exist,' said Rohan.

'There are certainly many things here to get surprised at,' said Robin. 'By the way this is Dragonock style timepiece.

Meanwhile Avni helped herself with some other timepieces as dragons did not really, please her.

'That is a silver band timepiece, Avni, it's popular among the school kids as the shiny silver colour on it really amuses them. They think, it is fantastic,' said Robin moving ahead towards the other shelves.

'I want to buy Drangonock style,' said Rohan looking hopeful that Robin would allow him.

'And what will we answer to mom, dad and Akriti that we brought it from another world,' said Avni raising her eyebrows.

'That is thoughtful of you,' said Rohan feeling dumb as he did not think of it.

'By the way, what would be our counterparts doing? The twins who are at home…' said Avni wondering and she got an intuition that the other twins are troubling Akriti.

'Oh, come on Avni, we'll think later,' said Rohan pulling her hand as they followed Robin.

'Well, we will proceed to the next cottage, a space themed one,' said Robin as they stepped out of the first one. They went past a huge number of people who were moving with trolleys of purchased items. A small boy was crying loudly as his mother did not purchase what he wanted. 'You are too small to buy Jupiter digital timepiece,' roared the mother. Avni and Rohan understood that there are digital timepieces in one of the cottages of the store. They were desperate to see that.

'This is the space theme cottage- all the fascinating digital timepieces are found here,' said Robin smiling at all the people who bowed in front of him out of respect. The space themed cottage was entirely different and unbelievable one. There were large boxes aligned together near the walls which contained solar system planet replicas on which digital time was portrayed in big rectangular boxes. 'So, this is the replica of earth as it is blue in colour and country maps can be seen as well,' said Rohan. 'This is really unbelievable.' He was thrilled at the sight of it.

'Ah, this is Jupiter. It is larger than others,' said Avni who seemed to be interested in space related things for the first time since anything which belonged to academics quite overburdened her. The cottage was spacious and the walls were not plain rather covered with solar system, stars and other celestial themed objects.

'The most famous digital timepiece is Saturn due to ring particles suspended around it,' said Robin and realised suddenly that he sounded more like a teacher.

'How are those things suspended around Saturn replica, I mean it is not real one, then how?' asked Avni curiously.

'Well, Avni, you seemed to be developing a lot of interest towards study, don't you nowadays?' said Robin. Avni and Rohan looked up at Robin and laughed hard.

'See that ring is supported with something, that's why,' he continued after their laugh was over.

'Hello Sir, how are you?' said a voice from behind.

'Oh, hello Aditi, I am fine, nice to meet you,' replied Robin to the small kindergarten aged girl. She was holding her father's hand, wearing a beautiful green dress. She smiled so cutely that Avni liked her instantly. 'How are you Mr Piyush?' asked Robin, politely to the little girl's father.

'I am fine, Mr Robin Spencer. Glad to meet you after a long time,' said the girl's father in a happy tone. 'Well can we talk later? I have, to purchase a nice digital space timepiece,' he said and marched ahead with his daughter.

'Every time he meets me, I only get to listen only one sentence- "well can we talk later?" Strange guy he is, that is why I remember him so well,' said Robin looking after that person who was busy purchasing digital clock. 'But that girl Aditi is sweet.'

Rohan and Avni just grinned and said nothing. As they were going to roam around further, a loud siren blew. For a split second the twins could not feel they had ears.

'What was that?' said Avni in a disgusted tone. Robin laughed at that.

'Avni, could you repeat, what you said just now? That horrible noise is echoing inside my ears and brain,' said Rohan.

'This is end-of-the-day-siren of this store. See, all people have started moving towards the exit gate, we should also go now,' said Robin hanging in the air.

'All people are requested to take your precious belongings and head towards exit gate. I hope your visit to our store was memorable. Thank you,' said the same voice who was announcing the instructions when Robin, Rohan and Avni were to enter the store.

After coming out of the exit gate, Rohan and Avni were quite delighted and cheerful with the experience of visiting an unbelievable and unimaginable place.

The weather had turned chillier and the sky was greyish-black.

The street lights were on and the road in front was half empty, very few cars passed with speed. Many people turned to the store's left side, towards the basement as they had parked their cars there. Rest went walking on the footpath.

'Now, before you start your questions, I want to tell that we will halt at Mr Jones' bungalow for few days now. It is empty,' said Robin and he took out the decoction pouch, mixed the ingredients, drank it and was back in human form. It was almost fifteen minutes past seven.

'Alright, but do we have to walk till then,' asked Rohan.

'Well, that's the hundredth question Rohan, I suppose,' said Robin patting Rohan on the back.

'Avni, if you have any questions, then just ask them all together, I will answer you both in a flow, I need not pause,' continued the Timekeeper, trying to sound funny.

'Avni was pretty interested in the surroundings and kept looking at the cars, shops and Timekeeper Store. It was still visible as they were standing exactly in front of it. Absent mindedly she answered 'No, I don't have any questions for time being. You may continue with your speech full of instruction.' Then she looked at the design of street light which fascinated her a bit.

'I do not give speeches full of instructions, of course you both are new to this World of Time. I need to tell everything,' replied Robin.

'Yes, we are your past-birth friends,' said Rohan mimicking Robin and laughed whole heartedly.

Robin didn't laugh rather spoke seriously-

'Leaving aside all these jokes, let me make you recollect that our main motive is to defeat Capvile and has ambition. Hope so Tara has collected some information about his next move. Take this decoction, it will directly transport us to Mr Jone's bungalow at Champions Street, number 22. Do not ask what the decoction contains, it's a complete secret for reaching a house and that is my innovation…'

The twins did not counter question and followed Robin's Instructions.

The trio took the decoction and after a spit second, they found themselves in front of a bungalow. They were at Champions Street, bungalow number 22.

'My palm is the key for this locked gate,' said Robin unlocking the black iron gate of Mr Jones' bungalow.

But Avni and Rohan were engrossed in observing the surroundings. The street was half empty and lights were on. Mr Jones' bungalow was no so large. But it looked entirely clean. 'Well maintained, isn't it?' said Rohan. 'Yes,' replied Avni pursing her lips as she felt a cold shiver.

Rohan put his hands in his jumper pocket and looked at Robin and felt that his facial expression was rather colder than the weather.

Robin was leaning over the gate losing his patience.

'Are we planning to come in or want to take a short trip over the street? We do not have time, do not waste it, tomorrow morning we have lot of work,' said the Timekeeper, earnestly and went up the small staircase of the bungalow and went in.

Rohan felt enraged. 'It's alright Rohan,' said Avni. 'He is the Timekeeper and we should respect him. He wants our support in this mission and remember that we have agreed for that.'

Rohan nodded a bit annoyingly. Both went inside.

'I am sorry, I shouldn't have talked to you like that. But being a Timekeeper, I have so many responsibilities aligned,' said Robin patting Rohan.

'There is no sorry in friendship,' said Rohan looking at the ceiling pretending to ignore the situation.

The bungalow was pretty clean from inside.

'There are no flashy wall papers, it is the monochromatic colour theme which I like the most and the paintings too are so beautiful,' said Robin.

The drawing room was attractive because of the simplicity maintained. There was a long staircase, connected to upper floor. 'Every furniture, every artefact is clean, well maintained and tidy,' said Avni as they returned to the kitchen after visiting other rooms of the bungalow.

'Yes, Mr Jones is a disciplined man. He lives in New Clockhist city which is about five kilometres from here,' said Robin pulling the dining table chair in the kitchen.

'Robin, the weather is cold here, but I do not see any black clouds or rain. Is it that this planet does not receive rains. Well, I will not be surprised to know that,' said Rohan shivering.

'No, the rains arrive sometime in mid-July every year,' said Robin.

'And you usually live in Clock Hill tower, hanging rather, so do you use any protection shield during rainy season?' asked Avni feeling proud to ask a sensible question.

'Yes of course, Avni. I do use my decoction for that,' replied Robin grinning wide.

'Aren't we hungry guys? He continued.

'What do you two want to eat, I will arrange that with my special decoction of Cardamom, Black Pepper and Peach flower extract.'

'My word!' said Rohan. 'If that's the case then I would prefer white sauce pasta. I hope people at the World of Time know what is pasta?'

'Yes, Rohan ninety-nine percent of the dishes in our world are similar to yours, to be precise,' replied the Timekeeper.

'Then I will have the same too,' replied Avni excitedly.

'Alright, we all will enjoy pasta in dinner today,' said Robin, mixing Cardamom powder, Black Pepper and Peach flower in a special pink liquid altogether in small glass and then he poured it on three plates kept in front of them muttering something softly which sounded like 'white sauce pasta.'

Avni was eager to ask a few questions before she helped herself with the tempting and delicious dinner and she started with her series of queries – 'Is there something different in the food cooked here which I can't notice? And does Timekeeper eat, really? Don't you think, pasta is not enough, I am starving!'

Rohan stopped midway while eating and both Robin and Rohan looked at her in amazement. 'She's got a point,' said Rohan.

'There are not many differences in the food, it's quite similar, as I have tasted food on your planet at the food restaurants. And yes, I do eat even though I am the Timekeeper,' said Robin in a little frustrated tone. 'I will get some chocolate cake for the dessert, don't worry,' he added further and this way all the questions were answered.

They enjoyed their dinner thoroughly with jokes and many more silly questions asked by Avni and then returned to the drawing room.

'We did not bring our belongings,' said Rohan looking down at his shoes which looked old and unclean. He needed a new pair.

'Need not worry about that, I will arrange important accessories for the time being. Now, the chit chats apart, tomorrow we all need to wake up at 6 am sharp. As you know we will meet Tara at Mr Ajay's house and discuss what is to be done ahead. This mission is going to be really significant. Things will work well, I am sure,' said Robin nodding his head as they paced down the hall slowly.

'All this seems mystery to you, yes, there are certain situations when we do not get the answers to anything. At times I feel the same too. I can understand your state of mind Rohan and Avni but do not worry you will understand things gradually,' said Robin Spencer.

'Of course, Robin, we trust you, we met you only few hours ago without the slightest idea of all this, but what I feel as if we three are always together and know each other since a long time,' said Rohan patting Robin on the back.

'Well, guys, I feel the atmosphere has become too serious, just chill, don't be stressed, only enjoy the journey,' said Avni sounding delightful.

The trio smiled at each other and the twins went to sleep in the ground floor rooms which were equally spacious as the hall. Robin turned back to his original Timekeeper form and hung on the wall opposite to a painting, using his decoction. He also slept peacefully but his tick-tock sound went on. A still silence fell in Mr Jones bungalow and soon everyone was in deep sleep after a long, tiring and surprising day.

Royal Pine 66

Avni woke at five minutes past six. She looked out of window in her room putting the curtains aside. The sun was not that bright, the sky was in shades of orange. The air was cold. She saw a bungalow on the other side and its windows were closed. The small road in between both houses, was empty. She felt something different and had forgotten that she was in World of Time. She still could not recollect about yesterday and went to grab her 'only-for-school-purpose' mobile to check if any notification was there about a day off in school due to rains. She turned around and finally realised.

'How stupid I am! I did not realise...' she said to herself and went muttering.

At around 6.30 am, two sleepy heads, Rohan and Avni were at the breakfast table, they were still half asleep. Eyes heavy with tiredness. Robin was in human manifestation again and noticed that the twins were still too lazy to wake up completely. He clicked his right-hand fingers twice and a shrieking alarm rang which made the twins jump and both sat upright staring at Robin.

'No wonder, you can ring an alarm being the Timekeeper,' said Rohan rubbing his eyes.

'Don't you have the habit of waking up early and studying, sleepy heads,' said Robin pulling a chair for himself.

'We wake up early every day, but not for studying! Do you really think, Robin, that we study? We are not like our sister,' said Avni shaking her head.

'Alright, that was just a joke, let us have a good breakfast for a good day,' said Robin taking out his decoction pouch.

'When you arrived here at the table with sleepy eyes, I was noting down a few important things in my diary,' said Robin as he gulped down a glass of hot chocolate.

Rohan was busy munching on his sandwiches but tried to ask hastily – 'What important thing?'

Avni was unwilling to eat her breakfast so early, howbeit tried hard to eat it and listened to Robin.

'First when we meet Tara, we'll ask about the information she received about Capvile. Second, we need to search a little further about Capvile's whereabouts. Third we need to make a quick move on the clues given by Tara. Fourth if our plan fails to trace the alchemist, Tara's backup plan needs to be implemented,' said Robin reading out the points from his diary.

'This is my favourite and secret pocket diary which I always keep in my pocket, to jot down important things. The amazing fact is that, it is an endless diary though it looks normal from outside, it has infinite pages,' he said in low whisper, giggling.

'Being the Timekeeper, you should remember what we must do ahead, right? Then why this diary,' said Avni trying not to laugh.

'That makes me more systematic,' said Robin drinking his last sip of hot chocolate.

A sumptuous breakfast really helped them to a great extent to feel energised. Rohan was tying his shoe lace tightly taking extra care of shoes provided by Robin. He was anxious and constantly thought about meeting Mr Ajay, the great journalist and Miss Tara.

Robin was writing something in his pocket diary sitting on the couch in drawing room. Avni was wondering hard that why on earth, they were going so early to meet them. She looked at her watch, it was 7:10 am. She was getting impatient with every second.

'I am done with another pending work of mine, guys, let's go now,' said Robin hurriedly.

They stepped out in the yard and opened the large iron gate. The sky was much brighter now and a faint cool breeze of air was blowing.

'This fresh air acts as source of motivation for me,' said Robin taking a deep breath to the feel the air.

The twins nodded their heads and gyrated in all directions only to find a plump woman in a blue dress who was watering the plant in great haste in her garden. She looked a bit tensed and wore a frown on her face. She looked up suddenly and saw the trio standing outside Mr Jones' bungalow. She did not smile at all and continued watering her plants.

'She is Ms Maya, always under some stress, you will never find her smiling,' said Robin. 'Anyways, now we are heading to Royal Pine 66 which is Mr Ajay's house. We will go by a taxi,' he said looking out for a taxi on the empty road.

'Do you expect any taxi arriving here at this time of morning? And do you have the money?' asked Rohan wonderingly.

'That is why I asked you to wake up early so that we need not struggle at last moment to find taxi and yes, I have the money. I have the right to arrange it from the bank. They have a special service for that,' replied Robin looking far at the end of road for a sign of taxi.

'Wow that's an advantage of being a Timekeeper,' said Avni mockingly for which Rohan giggled for about half a minute.

'Only in case of emergency, I do that -oh! Luckily, we have a taxi here. Good gracious,' said Robin happily and waved at the approaching taxi.

Robin showed his left palm and said 'Royal Pine 66' briskly. The driver was astonished and at the same time said – 'Hello Sir, please take the seat.'

It was a blue taxi. Avni and Rohan felt strangely odd to be seated in it as the taxi sped up very quickly on the Champions Street ahead. All three were seated behind and the driver was occasionally staring at Robin through the inside mirror.

Robin ignored him, since other things were more important to him than paying attention to people. He looked at the house and trees which passed with speed, but absent mindedly as he was constantly thinking about the 25th hour and Capvile. Avni and Rohan looked at the tall buildings, bungalows and trees of the beautiful Clockhist City.

Everything seemed normal to them, like Mumbai City -people, shops, roads, cars, almost all things were similar but at an instant they simultaneously felt different since they dearly missed their family.

The taxi went straight on the long road and finally took a left in a wide lane where several bungalows were aligned one after the other like houses on Champions Street. The taxi slowed and the driver shot one last look from the mirror at Robin and said – 'Sir, we have reached Royal Pine 66,' and he looked stiff scared.

The trio got down the taxi and Robin paid the money to the driver and said- 'try to be punctual and honest in your work, then you won't be afraid of me. Respect time and always remember that.' The driver nodded.

'Yes sir, sure. Thank you,' he said and drove ahead through the lane.

Finally, the trio was standing outside Mr. Ajay, the famous journalist's bungalow. It was a mixture of light yellow and off-white colour. The central door was brown and made of wood. It had two stone-brown pillars on either side as support.

One pillar had the name of bungalow stamped on it as – 'Royal Pine,' in beautiful, golden colour and below it was written – 'Mr Ajay Chauhan' in white. Outside the humungous iron gate were two security personnels who looked vigilant which was quite obvious since they were guarding the house of a famous journalist. They immediately approached the trio with stern looks just to say- 'why you children are standing here?'

'Well, I am the Timekeeper, Robin Spencer,' said Robin showing his miniature clock on the palm.

Immediately their facial expressions visibly changed and both the guards politely bowed in front of Robin and then one of them opened the front gate.

Avni, Rohan and Robin entered in the wide yard of the house.

Rohan felt delighted as he was standing there. He himself couldn't understand, but his mood was quite pepped up, probably his inner self was damn excited to be a part of this and while he thought all of that Robin had turned into his Timepiece manifestation and at the next moment a woman appeared from the backside of bungalow. She was tall and had a sweet smile on her face. She approached the trio who were still standing there. Robin and the lady exchanged a warm smile. The lady looked quite sophisticated. She had dark brown eyes and short hair like Avni and was wearing light jewellery. Her face was slightly wrinkled

'Good morning, Mrs Chauhan, meeting you after many days. How are you?' asked Robin lucidly.

'I am fine Robin Spencer. What about you? I am sure you must be busy with your secret missions,' said the lady in a sweet tone.

'Yes, I am good, bit busy with few things,' said Robin nodding his head.

'She glanced at the twins standing perplexed and spoke – 'Are you Avni and Rohan? I met you so many years ago and after that –

Robin interrupted– 'Yes, they are the twins and for your information, Mrs Chauhan they were reborn on Earth.' He gyrated his eyes as if concealing something and Rohan observed that. Avni was still looking at the Lady- 'May I know who you are?' she asked directly.

'This is Mrs Sunaina Chauhan, wife of Mr Ajay Chauhan. She is also a journalist, but she left the job few years ago to follow her passion of cooking and baking. She now owns a business of cakes,' said Robin.

'By the way I forgot to escort you three in. Come along with me,' said Mrs Chauhan with a welcome gesture. 'Now you need not worry, you three are going to stay at our house.'

Rohan looked bewildered and thought in mind – 'How does she know us and what is Robin trying to conceal as he interrupted Mrs Chauhan while she was speaking,' and then they followed Robin and Mrs Chauhan, inside the house. They entered the large living room of the bungalow. It was twice the size of Mr Jones' bungalow and even more luxurious than that.

The twins found out an astonishing difference in that house. The walls of the great living room weren't painted normally. They were all sponge painted with miniature timepieces in colour of orange, yellow and light green. There were no paintings and wall hangings but various kinds of wall clocks were hanging from one wall to another. Few could be recognised as Rose Essence, Dragonock style and Silver Band timepieces of the *Timekeeper's Store*. The furniture was stylish yet traditional. Having a look at the house after so many days made Robin happy and he went through the air as he was in his Timekeeper form, to meet Mr Ajay and Miss Tara as they were seated on the sofa having a profound discussion over something.

Mrs Chauhan also headed forward with a smiling face Avni and Rohan dragged their feet hard but they seemed to be flabbergasted oddly.

'Good morning, Mr Ajay and Tara. You both seem to be having a great discussion over something,' said Robin excitedly. Mr Ajay and Tara looked up in the air and smiled together.

'Hello Robin, what's up!' said Miss Tara as she got up to give a hi-five to Robin who was in the air.

'Look who is here Tara, your two very old friends- Avni and Rohan!' exclaimed Mrs Chauhan as she approached the dining table in the hall pouring water from the jug in the large glasses kept there.

'Old friends?' whispered Avni. 'I don't remember anything from my past birth, do you remember by any chance, Rohan?'

'No, I don't. But I remember the photo Robin had showed us at our home. She was there in that photo with us,' said Rohan in a very low voice.

'This is a unique mystery,' said Avni widening her eyes a bit.

'Hey, hello Avni and Rohan! What are you whispering to each other? Come in fast,' said Tara walking up to them.

Tara Chauhan was the one and only daughter of Mr Ajay Chauhan, the most famous journalist in the city of *Clockhist*. She worked as a detective for her father to unleash the dark secrets of people. She was still not a certified detective yet, but enjoyed her job thoroughly for her father and Robin Spencer. To be an authorised detective in World of Time, one needed three certifications from different existing organisations. By nature, Tara was honest and at the same time a bit mischievous. An avid reader of books and a big-time foodie too. She was not as pretty as her mother but resembled her father much more and looked smarter than anyone else.

The twins went along with her towards the large sofa. 'Good morning, Mr Ajay. Hello Tara,' said Avni sounding friendly as she shook hands with Tara.

'Hello everyone,' said Rohan nervously.

Mrs Chauhan arrived with a tray of glasses full of water and said in a cheerful tone- 'Take a seat, my dears, why are you both standing? Robin, I won't ask you to sit coz you're still in the air,' and everyone gave a shot of laughter for this statement except Mr Ajay who looked serious. Anyone could hardly expect him to laugh even on the craziest jokes.

Avni and Rohan took a seat nervously and looked a bit uncomfortable. New people, new atmosphere and most importantly a new world where things were different but strangely similar at the same time.

'I will get something to eat for you all,' said Mrs Chauhan and marched towards the kitchen.

Tara observed the twins and said- 'Don't be so uncomfortable, probably you don't remember anything from your past birth. Yes, that's the reason. In fact, I didn't believe the fact that you both were reborn on another planet, but then Robin broke this news to us after discovering this...'

Robin who had lowered himself a bit in the air suddenly shook his head and Tara looked at him curling her lips.

Rohan saw that and immediately tried to ask – 'What is it...'

'Nothing, we may discuss these things later,' said Robin putting an end to the conversation.

Mr Ajay was writing down something in his diary and pondering hard so he didn't listen to either of them. He then looked up and spoke earnestly – 'Tara can we have a discussion over our mission. It is the most important thing right now.'

'Yes of course dad,' replied Tara.

Robin cleared his throat and started to speak first by moving his little fingers of his small protruding hands- 'listen to me carefully Rohan and Avni. We are going to confront a dangerous and dark natured person, Capvile, whose mission is to create a 25th hour of time which is certainly against the law of nature. How did he get to this idea, no one knows and you very well remember being told all this by me, right?'

'Yes, we do,' said the twins together.

'The alchemist Capvile is a stupid fellow, always trying to achieve some unconventional feats. His procedures of experimenting, his ambitions and his whereabouts are always a mystery to everyone which is difficult to decode. I have come up with the information that he has a few people around him who try to sneak in secret chemicals and secret decoctions to him,' said Tara. 'If he succeeds in this peculiar experiment, its going to affect the cycle of nature first of all and the outer appearance of Robin in critical ways.' She paused.

Robin's eyes looked watery. It seemed unusual for the twins as they hadn't seen a timepiece having eyes and crying over something.

There was a silence of few seconds but Avni spoke in between- 'Yes disrespecting time isn't something good.'

Rohan stared at his sister as he couldn't believe her saying 'disrespecting time isn't good' because she herself was so unpunctual and irregular in doing things unlike their elder sister Akriti.

Robin started sobbing and rubbed his eyes with his small protruding hands. The tick-tock of the seconds hand inside him and his sobbing went in a rhythm together.

'Robin, we are with you,' said Avni in an encouraging tone.

'Yes, thank you,' said Robin rubbing his eyes again. 'Time is not something to be messed up with,' he continued in a heavy voice. 'Time itself creates magic in life if valued and revered. But people like Capvile don't understand at all. We all know, how dark minded he is.'

Tara continued- 'His ambitious nature to carry out unconventional yet stupid experiments have expelled him out of so many great research organisations in the past and now the fact that no reputed research organisation supports his destructive ideas, he has probably joined a research centre which allows independent alchemists and scientists to invent their own scientific ideas.'

'And it's not as easy as we think to destroy his experiment,' said Mr Ajay as he shook his head. 'Tara has got something to tell you all apart from all this, by the way, regarding Capvile,' and he looked at his daughter to continue ahead.

Tara nodded her head and said in a very firm tone – 'Yes dad. What I have got to know from my secret sources is that, Capvile is going to take help of a *decoction-book* for his work. Anyways, what you three need to do is find out the solutions for the clue which I will go on passing to you as I get the information. This mission can turn into an intense one if it has to, so we need to be careful because Capvile will also trace us back if he gets aware about our motives and that is quite certain to happen. Did you all get that?'

'Yes Tara, we got it. We have to work on the clues given by you,' said Avni with a very sincere look for the first time.

'We will also try to find out about the *decoction* book,' said Rohan who looked extremely curious to know about it.

Robin felt proud for an instance about his dear friends and about him as well because he had persuaded the twins up till here and now, they agreed upon things smoothly without questioning.

'I knew you both would agree quickly,' said Robin confidently.

'Go on,' said Rohan.

'Tara, please show the video footage of Capvile which you had managed to get with the help of *Informer Spy*,' said Robin lowering him selves even more in the air.

Mr Ajay was watching everyone silently sitting on his couch and said– 'As far as I know you both twins possess a special talent of reading minds, isn't it? Well, you had that in your blood in your past birth. Just observe the video footage being showed to you carefully and try to read Capvile's mind, if possible, by any chance,' and he straightened his spectacles hopingly that their first step will somewhat help them.

'What? We need to read his mind? And is this the first step of our mission, really?' asked Rohan hastily looking confused. He had expected something thrilling like deciphering a clue or code just like the suspense movies but unfortunately the twins had to showcase their unique talent of reading minds. They usually discussed within themselves even if they had read someone's mind and amused each other playfully. But now their unique talent had got a chance to work professionally for a mission.

'Yes of course, Rohan,' said Tara opening her dad's laptop kept on the small table in front of her.

Avni seemed excited so didn't ask anything and tried to put in her head to see the laptop brand written on top. But frowned in an instant because the brand wasn't known to her and she remembered that this is the World of Time and the companies along with brands would be different here. Rohan immediately pulled her apart and widened his eyes angrily.

Tara started to show the video footage of Capvile. The twins had seen him for the first time. The dark minded Capvile had a bulgy and thick face and greenish eyes. A long, pointed nose added to his more than a vamp like face. He was in a long blue coat and round blue hat. There was a dark element in him definitely which reflected on his face.

The twins opened their mouths wide in shock and looked horrified for a moment. He typically looked like a vamp in those suspense movies to them.

Capvile was sitting on a huge velvet red chair in a circular room. There were many people in the circular room apart from them who were sitting on round tables facing Capvile and listening to him. After few seconds Capvile got up from his velvet chair and paced in the room around the people instructing them something. But nothing could be heard as it was a silent video.

'Can you zoom and pause the video a little bit, Tara?' asked Rohan.

'Yes, why not,' said Tara.

The twins studied Capvile's face closely. They tried to sneak past his mind to know what all dark secrets his mind possessed. Robin, Tara and Mr Ajay looked at the twins hopefully and expected an answer from them.

The twins pondered hard and studied Capvile's face for few minutes but couldn't do so.

'Difficult. Very difficult to sneak past his mind. I am unable to make out anything,' said Avni scratching her forehead. 'Can you read his mind, Rohan?' she asked hopingly.

'Well, frankly telling, even I am unable to,' said Rohan shrugging his shoulder.

'Hmm…well I thought so before that Capvile must have done something so that nobody could read his mind and nobody could reach his secret working place,' said Mr Ajay staring at the paused video footage.

'Which place is this? Were you able to find out through any hint Tara?' asked Robin thoughtfully.

Tara stood up from her place and started pacing here and there saying, 'No, I tried hard but couldn't find any clue. I have asked *Informer Spy* to keep on dropping hints about their secrets and if possible, get me the direct information which is, quite difficult. It's not that easy, to get all that in this case.'

Robin gave a sigh and put his round clock-head, down in stress and thought, 'how is everything going to be sorted out?'

'Robin, you are not an ordinary being, why don't you use your powers with the help of decoctions and whatever other thing which is possible? Then it would be just a matter of few seconds and Capvile will lament for his experiment failure,' said Rohan in one go and breathed heavily to stop.

'Of course, I am the Timekeeper, but this is a different situation. Here my powers are of no use, don't you think I might have tried earlier in my best possible ways to confront him alone? I don't know what evil plans he's thinking of!' said Robin in a slight rage.

'Sorry, Robin. I didn't mean to-

'That's alright, Rohan. I got angry with...sorry', said Robin patting Rohan with his little hands through air.

'All the discussions aside. Gather around the table for a sumptuous breakfast,' came bursting in Mrs Chauhan with a large tray of several tasty dishes. She was smiling widely and arranged everything on the table quickly for all of them.

'But Mrs Chauhan, we had our breakfast before we came here,' said Avni eyeing the dishes as her mouth watered a bit. 'Wow, you sound so innocent as if you don't want to eat anything,' whispered Rohan in his twin sister's ear, grinning wide.

They all quickly settled around the table and helped themselves with quick breakfast. Robin didn't eat much as he looked a bit tensed and pondered hard. Even if Avni and Rohan had their breakfast before and now as they were eating for the second time within such a short period, it didn't seem though, as they emptied their dishes very fast without uttering a word.

Tara was satisfied and felt energised, so she complimented her mom-'It was fantastic, mom. I liked the chocolate muffin with chocolate chip toppings...'

What's the plan?

Later, that same afternoon, they were still discussing about their mission but it had turned a bit monotonous since none of them had a clue of what must be done next. So, Mr Ajay had started working on another exciting news leaving aside this.

'The famous singing band, *Rule out*, is arriving in the City of Clockhist to promote their new song. That is interesting,' said Mr Ajay reading out aloud the piece of news to his daughter.

'My word, that's a famous group, dad. Definitely you are going to interview them, isn't it?' asked Tara sounding excited.

'Yes, dear,' replied Mr Ajay. 'But if I am busy with other stuff then I have to ask someone else to do it.'

Avni and Rohan listened to the conversation and looked confused. Robin, who had turned back to his human form approached them and said- 'Well, you might be wondering that how come Mr Ajay can work for two different departments of interviewing celebrities and decoding the secret missions of dark minded people, isn't it? He is the most famous and excellent journalist who can handle different departments. Clockhist Enigma newspaper had decided long ago to promote him as head of several departments.'

'Come along with me and sit here. I am preparing a map of Clockhist city,' said Robin sitting on the dining table in the hall.

'For what?' asked Avni pulling a chair for herself.

'Do you think that I only show the time and do nothing else. Hanging on the Hill Tower, what else does Robin Spencer do...' he said taking out a pen and straightening a rolled parchment kept on the table.

'I need to make a fresh hand-made map everyday of different cities and pour my special decoction on it to test whether everyone is revering time or not. Today I need to do it for Clockhist city. That's not a tedious work for me at all definitely. By doing so I will come to know which block or street or house or building isn't much concerned for time and then I have to go to the respective place and teach them a lesson so that they won't repeat this in future. Because as told by me earlier, time is not something to be messed with. Time is a wonderful resource if used wisely and understood deeply. Did you get that?'

'Alright. But what's the secret decoction used for doing this work?' asked Avni who was in awe after listening to this new piece of news broken in by the Timekeeper himself.

'And how do you come to know about who is to be punished? I mean some graphical data or...' said Rohan raising his eyebrows.

Before Robin could answer, Tara's mobile phone rang loudly and everyone jumped at once. Mr Ajay who was sitting at his work desk in the same living room just moved his eyes from his office laptop and gave a slide glance at his daughter as if to say- 'why did you disturb when I am doing something important?'

She picked up the phone (which was lying on the sofa) and answered. The call went on for two-three minutes and Robin, Rohan and Avni were listening eagerly, trying to make out the conversation.

'Are you sure about the secret code? If yes then I need to start working on it with my team,' said Tara with a serious look on her face. 'This is a very crucial information, Informer Spy. Thank you so much and do update me with every information you receive.' She dropped the call.

Tara cleared her throat and spoke –

'After gathering all the information and history of Capvile, I had reckoned that there is a secret way of conversation between Capvile and his teammates and that speculation was right. I have finally come to know about the secret code which Capvile and his team uses frequently. It consists of a digit and five letters. Well, it can mean a place, thing, anything in short.'

'Tell the code, Tara,' said Robin desperately.

'I am coming to that, Robin be patient,' she replied.

'The code is 3 R-A-D-L-Y.'

There was a moment of silence in the air, then Mr Ajay spoke sternly- 'Tara and Robin Spencer, you must begin with the work now. Start solving the clue. Of course, Tara, you know what and how it has to be done.'

'Should we go the garden area for discussing further?' asked Rohan who wanted to explore garden area and help Tara and Robin in solving the code.

'No, Rohan, we will go to my library to solve the clue and also try to collect some information from some books,' said Tara.

Avni and Rohan glanced at each other and then at Robin who had already started moving. 'Where is it?' asked both the twins.

'Upstairs,' replied Robin Spencer taking the stairs exactly on the right of the large couch area.

The twins entered the special 'Golden Library of Tara.' It was perfectly arranged with typical book shelves on left side wall. The book shelves were embedded. In the centre was a shiny dark-brown wooden table and a leather chair. At the back of it was a wooden sofa set which gave the room unique look and the entire set up was impressive.

'This is where I usually work when at home. It's a perfectly quiet place,' said Tara, emptying some book shelves and looking for books. 'But dad likes to work on his desk in the living room. He rarely comes here,' she said shrugging her shoulder.

'Robin, use some decoction and arrange three leather chairs. I don't have extra chairs here,' said Tara settling down on her large chair.

Robin took his decoction pouch, poured blue ink and a black powder from the pouch to glass. The mixture boiled and he spilt it down on the floor. Three big leather chairs appeared, the next moment.

'My special decoctions,' said Robin smiling wide. Rohan and Avni nodded together, smiling too.

Tara took a sheet of paper and wrote the code on it with a blue pen.

'I doubt that this code stands for some initials of certain words. It is difficult to crack but not impossible,' said Tara staring at the sheet of paper.

'Certainly, Tara. Right now, Capvile has only one motive- to create the 25th hour of time,' said Robin playing with the paper weight kept on the table.

'And this code surely contains the secret of his plan. Am I right?' said Rohan glancing at Tara and Robin alternatively. Avni raised her eyebrows and patted her brother on the back as she agreed to his statement.

'Absolutely Rohan you have got the right point, said Tara. 'These are few books related to time, which I am giving to you both, Rohan and Avni.'

She handed three books to the twins titled as – '*History of Time*', '*The Great Facts*' and '*Robin Spencer*'

The twins glanced at the third book which was authored by Robin Spencer, the Timekeeper himself and it was an autobiography.

'You write books?' asked Avni questioningly. 'Yes, I do,' replied Robin still playing with the paper weight. 'I have written hundreds of them.'

Tara did not pay attention to conversation rather she was concerned about the clue and its solution. She wrote down a few points on blank paper and said – 'Read this, you two.' Avni took a piece of paper in her hand and Rohan put his head into it, as both of them read aloud whatever was written on paper-

- Third chapter of 'History of Time' contains names of places where some history was created related to time and unknown secrets related to time.
- 'The Great facts' has a last chapter based on 24 hours of time.

'Don't read anything from my book,' said Robin and he snatched the piece of paper and tore the bottom part where the last point was written by Tara regarding his book.

'Why, what happened Robin? Asked Rohan. Sorry, I can't answer you now,' replied Robin sternly.

'Robin, you are concealing something from us,' said Avni. 'Isn't it Rohan?'

'Yes, even I have observed that,' said Rohan.

'Many times, I felt, you tried to conceal something. Robin, you must tell us whatever you are…'

'I will tell when the right time comes,' replied Robin even more sternly. 'Do not force me, you need to listen to the Timekeeper.'

'Guys for time being, you can go through the other two books,' said Tara ending the argument between Robin and Rohan.

Avni opened the third chapter of 'History of Time.'

Rohan also put his head in the book. Both were reading it together.

'Rohan, you can read *The Great Facts*. Try to save time and work smartly,' said Robin handing them the book.

'But we do everything together, Robin,' replied Avni smiling wide. Robin grinned, back too.

'Then read it aloud, one of you,' he said.

'History of Time' seemed very interesting to them. The third chapter which they were reading contained names of places like 'Clockhist' (city where they were staying currently), 'Timezz', 'Hourland', 'John's time' etc.

Avni read it aloud to which Robin and Tara were listening eagerly.

At the very end, a line was given on page fifty-two of that book which made Tara and Robin thump on the table together, as Avni read it.

'The Decoction factory in city of Clockhist is a famous place without any doubt. The city was formed in the year 1531, it still enjoys great tourist attraction. The readymade decoctions made here are used by the people of World of Time in extreme emergency situations. Otherwise, one cannot. Only the Timekeeper-Robin Spencer can use it as and when required.' Avni took a pause and glanced at Robin to which he gave a nod.

'Wait Avni,' said Tara Rotating a pen in her hand. 'Robin, I think you understood, what we have to do next'.

'Yes, we should immediately go to the Decoction factory,' said Robin. But its late now. It is 5'o clock in the evening and now the weather is turning cold. We can go there tomorrow in the morning.'

'Okay then, we four and Informer Spy will report to the Decoction factory tomorrow at sharp 9 am,' said Tara getting up and placing the books properly on the shelf.

'We can look for solution of our problem there. May be the secret code contains something which is there in Decoction factory,' said Robin. Mrs. Chauhan entered the room.

'Can we have these discussions later? I think we all should have some tea and snacks now. The weather is turning cold, some hot tea will surely help,' she said patting Avni on her back.

'Yeah, sure Mom. I am damn hungry,' said Tara who hurriedly went down stairs for tea-time.

'Your dad has gone for an important meeting,' said Mrs Chauhan bringing in the tray full of tea pot and tasty snacks tray as they all settled at the dining table of the beautifully large 'Royal Pine 66' bungalow. 'He may return tomorrow. He went instantly after receiving call from his journalist friend,' she said.

'Alright,' said Robin passing the plate to Rohan.

'And that's extremely delicious, Mrs Chauhan,' said Avni munching on chocolate cookies. 'I am a big-time foodie and what can be better snack than your cookies Mrs Chauhan. I just love them now,' she said excitedly.

'Of course, they are the best,' said Tara sipping some hot tea and munching cookies simultaneously. 'By the way, Robin, have you read the new book by Niti Sinha? It's just awesome,' she said smilingly.

'I haven't, but I suppose it is all about Dragons, isn't it?' said Robin eating the last bit of his chocolate cookie. 'I haven't even seen it.'

'You don't know the title also?' asked Tara.

Rohan and Avni looked at each other and shrugged their shoulder as they knew nothing about the people of World of Time.

'No, but when I met her last time, she seemed damn interested in Dragons. She kept asking me about them and I answered all I could. Do you guys know, dragons and monsters really existed on our planet before humans came. I have met them,' said Robin drinking tea.

Avni, Rohan and Tara stopped midways eating their snacks and gaped at Robin.

'You have met them? Dragons?' asked Rohan, who looked dumb founded.

'As I have told you before, when I was born, I just opened my eyes and found myself on Hill Tower, hanging there. This happened a long time ago, I found a baby dragon walking in front of me, on the ground.'

Avni, Tara and Rohan broke in a riot of laughter. They all were laughing, even Mrs Chauhan was smiling. Rohan was about to spill his tea on the table but luckily Avni poked him laughing and he put the mug on the table.

'Surprisingly Robin, the Hill Tower and Dragons existed together. Was there no forest? This Clockhist city had developed before humans stepped in here, do you want to say that?' asked Rohan giggling.

'Yes', answered Robin with a smile.

Everyone stopped laughing now and listened to the Timekeeper and his story with full curiosity.

'This is where the difference lies dear Rohan. World of Time had proper developed cities with roads, buildings and so many things. Humans stepped in later. Earth has the opposite case. Also, that Earth is a planet of humongous universe but World of Time exists invisibly on Earth itself. Of course, the dragons and monsters vanished as humans were born here,' said Robin still smiling. 'The baby dragon looked too cute when I saw it first, it was grey in colour...'

The laughter re-continued later for long as Robin kept describing the baby dragon and other monsters which he had met so far. But still Robin had the stress at back of his mind which constantly reminded him of twenty-fifth hour and the thought did not fade away whatsoever he tried to do to get rid of it.

The weather was turning colder and the dark black sky at night with twinkling stars looked beautiful. Robin, Rohan and Avni were standing at the large kitchen window, all three wondering about the happenings of past few hours.

'What must be our counterparts doing right now?' asked Avni who suddenly remembered about the pair of twins (Rohan and Avni's counterparts).

'I think they might be asleep by now,' replied Rohan.

'I feel the same,' said Avni since other parted twins and original twin pair felt the same when they thought of each other.

Robin was not interested in listening to them. He was first worried about the solution of secret code which they came to know from Tara's Informer Spy which is supposed to be used by Capvile and his team probably for the succession of his plan.

'What does 3-R-A-D-L-Y mean?' said Robin folding his hands, looking at the dark sky.

'Only this question is troubling me right now,' he continued.

'Avni and Rohan stopped thinking about other twin pair as Robin's question diverted their attention.

'We will come to know very soon Robin,' said Avni, sounding quite wise.

'Decoction factory is an important destination, we will not leave anything which comes across without inspecting it properly,' said Rohan.

Next day would be extremely important for Robin Spencer and he was eagerly waiting for it to arrive, spending a sleepless night pondering over the secret code.

Decoction factory

'I think, I left my decoction pouch on the living room table,' said Robin Spencer who was in his original manifestation and went inside the bungalow again before leaving for Decoction factory by car.

'Robin, value yourself,' said Avni and glanced sideways at Rohan and Tara who were already in the car and sat near the window with protruded heads, staring at Avni for her recent statement.

'Sorry, I meant-Robin, value time,' she changed her statement. 'Of course, I said that as he himself is time.'

Robin appeared with his decoction pouch, through the air. 'Settle down fast,' said Tara impatiently who was going to drive the car herself. Robin went inside the car through window and remained still in the air, his round head almost touching the roof of car. Mrs Chauhan waved at them standing at the gate and off they were taking the shorter route to main road.

Tara was speeding up the car a bit and her impatience was visible through that. Rohan kept his head leaned on the window staring at the drifting white clouds which were slowly making way for sunlight. Avni really seemed happy by the fascinating square houses and large buildings. She also remembered the 'Timekeeper Store' which they had visited right after meeting Mr. Ajay in the beautiful city of Clockhist.

Robin was not seated, rather he was touching inside roof of the car. He did not speak anything throughout their way to Decoction factory. He looked extremely nervous.

'Informer Spy will report there directly. We need to reach quickly. Its half past eight now, another half an hour and we will be right there.

At sharp 9 am they were at the entrance of Decoction factory. 'This is such a humongous door for a factory,' said Avni. 'That too wooden,' said Rohan with awed expressions.

The entrance was unique. A large thirteen feet wooden door of hickory brown shade was the first visible surprise for the twins.

'This is the entrance for the Timekeeper only,' said Tara looking at Robin who was in the air above nodding his head as he agreed to her. 'As he is a very important person for Decoction factory.'

'Wow Robin,' said Avni appreciating him. Robin just smiled and said nothing. He went closer to the door and did some hand gesture in the air. He put his palm on the top left of the large door. The door security system recognized the imprint of 'Timekeeper Hand.' As soon as he put his hand, there was an announcement that followed- 'The Timekeeper, Robin Spencer enters the factory.'

The door opened. Avni, Rohan, Tara and Robin crossed the entrance and to the twin's surprise, there were hundreds of people standing and bowing to the Timekeeper as he entered.

'Robin you are truly an important person,' said Rohan looking around at everyone.

'They respect time, dear Rohan,' said Robin in a soft voice.

'Really? I do not believe,' said Avni suspecting people around, thinking that they were faking it.

'Good morning, everyone. Please continue with your work,' said Robin and the people around dispersed as he spoke.

'Avni, dear, we have another surprise,' said Rohan in a hushed voice.

Avni who was busy observing people looked in the direction where Rohan was pointing.

At a distance of few meters in the front, there was an enormous black castle which was the main factory area.

The place where the twins, Robin and Tara were present had small square buildings. People were coming in and out of those small buildings, some were carrying pouches in hand and others empty handed.

The pouches were very similar to the one that Robin had.

'I will call Informer Spy,' said Tara taking out her mobile. 'Not picking up my phone,' she said after a few seconds.

'Coz, there he is,' said Robin, still in the air, pointing out to the spy who was approaching them from the side square building.

'Hello people, Hello Mr Robin Spencer, here is Informer Spy for your very crucial service,' said the new entrant in the group.

'Hello Informer Spy,' said Robin smiling.

'I hope you are good,' said Informer Spy calmly.

'We were absolutely fine until we got the news of Capvile,' said Tara frustratingly.

'Any more news on the mind?' She asked further.

'Of course,' replied Informer Spy, smiling slightly under his thin and long moustache. The new member was short and thin. He had a special talent of observing people passing by and speaking to someone at the same time. He did so while talking to Tara and Robin as his eyes rotated alternatively from the two to the surrounding crowd spread across the factory.

'Continue to speak, Informer,' said Robin desperately.

Informer Spy continued in the low voice-

'I went to Clockhist Spooky Cafe, yesterday, for a coffee in the evening. Next to my table there were three people sitting and discussing something. They were wearing large sunglasses and grey coloured hats. All the three men looked strangely same to me and I felt something fishy so I went near the newspaper stand, pretending, to read so that I could hear them.'

He took a pause to look at a man passing by, turned his head back and continued- 'They were discussing about Capvile.'

Robin who was hanging in the air, lowered himself a bit to listen to the latest news with utmost caution. 'And what did they say about him?' he asked even with more desperation.

'They were talking about Main-square of this decoction factory. Also, about the fourth Main-square. In between they talked in extremely low whispers, so I just observed the first person's lip movement over the newspaper which sounded like the name Capvile to me. Then they said that the Main-square and fourth Main-square's manufactured decoctions are important. For about five minutes this conversation was on and then three men conveniently finished their coffee and went away. I tried to ask the café manager about the three men but he was not aware about them except the fact that they visited the café sometimes.' Informer Spy finished telling the story.

'Did this happen after you gave the code word?' asked Tara folding her hands.

'Yes,' he replied, nodding his head.

'Tara, we should immediately go to both the squares and try to find out if Capvile and his team are trying to sneak out any decoctions for inception of the 25th hour,' said Robin, sounding tensed.

'Just a minute Robin,' said Tara rubbing her chin as she spoke. 'The facts we have gathered till now may obviously prove helpful to us. Let me recollect what we know…'

'First, we came across the fact that Capvile is planning to actualize the 25th hour. Second, we got to know that his team is using a code word 3RADLY for conversing. Third we decided to visit decoction factory for a trial as we thought of receiving some further hints. Fourth we came to know that few people in Clokchist Spooky Café were talking about decoction factory, means our visit to this crucial place will not be a waste. That is a fantastic thing!'

Robin heard all the points carefully and a question arose in his mind-'Did the people at the café use 3RADLY code at any time during their conversation?'

'Valid question, Robin,' said Tara.

Avni and Rohan, however chose to keep quiet and just listened.

'No, sir, they did not,' said Informer Spy.

'Hmm, I see... I think we should start our work without any further ado,' said Tara, looking at Robin, the Timekeeper's clock to check the time. It was half past nine. The second's hand was moving steadily in Robin Spencer.

'Yes, let's go to the black castle,' said Informer Spy.

The group of five went marching ahead towards the enormous black castle. 'Why do you call him Informer Spy?' asked Rohan questioningly to Tara. 'No name?'

Informer Spy overheard him saying that, so he replied – 'Being a spy, I have kept my original name secret.'

Rohan observed the spy along their way to castle. He was wearing a dark blue shirt and a red cap. What was more visible on his face was his confidence. His eyes had a different and a unique element which made him look intelligent and smart spy. Rohan felt impressed.

'Avni and Rohan, this is the entrance staircase of the Decoction factory which goes inside the castle,' said Robin as they climbed up.

'Alright but what are we going to do now?' asked Avni. 'How are we going to find solution for the secret code?'

'Even I am not sure about that,' said Robin.

They climbed up the grey staircase and the twins stood open mouthed for the two-hundredth time.

There were at least twenty people working with certain equipment in the factory. There was a long table in the large factory's Main-square. Every person standing was assigned various tasks with decoction manufacturing.

'Come on in, everyone, I will explain each step of the procedure of decoction manufacturing,' said Robin bending his head down to speak.

'Of course, Miss Tara and I am aware of it, but we would like to hear out from the Timekeeper,' said Informer Spy with a wide grin. 'Also let us see if we can sneak out some information from these workers regarding Capvile.'

'But we cannot ask them directly,' said Rohan raising his eyebrows.

'We have other ways to let out such secrets,' he replied in a low whisper and smiled.

'Robin spencer, the Timekeeper is here,' said a short heighted man who was supervising a furnace in the left corner.

The other people lifted their heads up. Many of them smiled and some said 'Hello Sir!'

'Do you need any decoction ingredient sir?' asked the furnace supervisor who was wearing a black protection helmet and green protection jacket.

'No, I am here to show this factory and the manufacturing process to my guests,' replied Robin as they all went to the left counter of Main-square.

Avni and Rohan looked very pleased to experience all this. They were quite excited to understand the decoction concept. The twins were not interested in studying but such kind of things surely fascinated them.

Robin started reciting the procedure.

'The first person standing here is working on a decoction which has steel extract in it. He is trying to file the steel stripes from steel plant,' he said.

'The stripes made of steel are having certain length and width,' continued Robin in an explanatory tone, looking at the twins to make them understand.

The person was filing the steel stripe with a medium sized equipment.

'The original size of the stripe is different so it needs proper measuring and cutting and then filing,' said Robin. 'The second person here is softening the steel with a special fire lighter,' he added further as they moved ahead.

Meanwhile Tara was simultaneously observing every person working there and listening to Robin. She was a good observant being a detective. If any suspicious personality met her, she would probably recognize with ease, so she kept an eye on everyone.

Robin was as well eyeing every person and he even asked the supervisor-

'Have you seen any suspicious person asking for decoction pouches? Something unusual in anyone which made you feel strange about that person?'

'No sir, I have not. But I do not know if another Main-square personnel of this factory has seen anyone like this,' replied the supervisor. 'Sorry for asking the venerable Timekeeper, may I know why sir?'

'You need not be sorry. But I have reasons which I cannot tell,' replied Robin.

'I doubt this supervisor himself. Tyring to be extra polite to Robin,' whispered Rohan to Avni which was overheard by Informer Spy. He burst in saying – 'I know the supervisor well. He is a good person. Don't form any opinion about him.' He sounded a bit annoyed.

'Can you tell me the list of decoctions and whatever else is made here at the Factory?' asked Tara. 'Something which we're not aware of.' She stood with folded hands, which was her usual gesture while doing her job.

The supervisor who was standing near the furnace instructed the assistant to keep an eye on the furnace, he approached the group of five who were waiting for answers from him.

'We make hundreds of decoctions ma'am and I have a list of them, if you want one, here it is,' said the supervisor while taking out a list which he handed to Tara.

'If you don't mind, can we keep this list?' asked Robin pointing his little finger towards the list.

'Yes sir, sure. As you say,' he replied.

Avni saw a person, working at the counter who gave a nasty smile after listening to the supervisor's statement. 'Doesn't respect Robin-that one,' she whispered to Rohan.

Tara went through the list quickly; it was quite long. She was trying to re-arrange certain facts in her mind and then she asked- 'Is there anything in the decoction factory which starts from the letter R?'

Robin glanced at her immediately as he understood what she wanted to ask.

Avni did not get the question so she scratched her head and she opened her mouth to speak, but Rohan whispered to her before that- 'The R in 3 RADLY code word.' She understood.

'Not exactly from R ma'am. But yes, we have *3 Rings Anti Decoction Library* in the factory,' replied the supervisor. 'It does not start with R but, a digit of course. The letter R follows it.'

'And here we have the answer,' said Robin with a satisfactory smile.

He looked pleasingly thrilled. So too Tara and the spy.

'Answer?' asked the supervisor, looking surprised. Tara quickly responded- 'Thank you so much, you have been a great help to us,' carrying the same satisfactory smile as Robin had.

Rohan too understood all that had been spoken, just now but his twin Avni could not. She had a blank expression on her face. They both followed Robin, Tara and the spy to *3 Rings Anti Decoction Library* which was very much in the castle as the supervisor told them.

The Card of Intimation

The answer for the code had been found out. 'If this is the answer then why didn't Robin and Tara think of it before?' asked Avni as they all turned a corner in the long passage inside the castle. She was now aware of the answer as Rohan told her while leaving the Main-square.

Robin heard what Avni said, so he calmly replied- 'Dear Avni, the name was changed from *Anti-Decoction Central Library* to *3 Rings Anti-Decoction* Library. We both weren't aware of it.'

The Informer Spy didn't speak at all on their way but Tara instructed him thrice to be watchful and alert. Robin and Tara both exchanged anxious looks. They got down a long staircase after walking in the passage.

There was the humongous *3 Rings Anti -Decoction Library*, with two large doors which were very much open. In went the group which still didn't have even half of the answers to their entire mission.

Although Robin being the Timekeeper knew how to handle difficult things and people but this was totally different. For the first time in life, he was far away from his Hill Tower for a long and he was not attending people to solve their time related issues and neither he could counsel the people who were careless about time and did not respect it. From the past few days two thoughts kept scuffling in his mind- the formation of 25th hour and its consequences.

'Have they renovated the library?' asked Tara wonderingly as they approached the library counter where Librarian was seated. But she was not there at the place. So, they waited.

'Seems to be renovated,' said Robin flying in the air. 'It's been seven months since I have been to the library and no one told me either, that's it's being renovated.'

Rohan was quick to respond to this and blithered impetuously- 'Nobody tells the Timekeeper and why is that so?'

Avni gave a sharp look to him. Robin replied with a smile- 'well it's not that necessary to inform every little thing going on in the World of Time to me.

Rohan didn't say anything but thought in his mind – 'Then why did you say that nobody told you?'

Avni recognised that and again gave a sharp look.

The Librarian returned. An extremely skinny lady. She walked in between the two large book shelves on either side slowly. Her face was highly pointed. She looked kind and gentle as she smiled at Robin while taking the seat. Avni liked her long velvet dress.

'Robin, it has been seven months, three days and ten hours since you have visited,' said the Librarian leaning forward and smiled and blinked her grey eyes.

'That's a very precise calculation of yours, Madam Lucy,' said Robin lowering down in the air. 'By the way, how are things going on. Do people visit the library these days?'

The Librarian gyrated her eyes from the twins, Tara, Informer Spy and then towards Robin very calmly and slowly. Then she replied- 'Things are of course the same. No change. Only the fact that this Library has changed a lot, its renovated.' She lifted her hands off and leaned back at the chair. 'And people are extremely busy to visit the library except a few who are very well constant…'

Robin repeated her last word and emphasised on it – 'constant?'

The Librarian put her hand on the mouth as if she had spoken something which she should not have. Robin and Tara observed that peculiar gesture. 'Why did you stop?' asked Tara.

'Robin,' emphasised the Librarian, 'Are you here to collect some information?'

'It's none of your business, Madam Lucy,' said Robin placidly.

'I have something with me which I am supposed to give you,' said the Librarian, hastily opening the drawer of her work desk. She took out a red coloured envelope and handed it to Robin. 'Open it Robin, right here.'

Robin checked the envelope's front and back side for it would have some reference or name written, but nothing was there. He opened it and found a red coloured card on which few words were calligraphed and he read everything in mind-

CARD OF INTIMATION

'The venerable Robin Spencer. I know, you must be desperately searching for ways to find out how I am going to generate the 25th hour of time. I am aware of the fact that Miss Tara Chauhan, the daughter of famous journalist Mr Ajay Chauhan is with you. Also, the twins from the planet of Earth, your very dear friends, are helping you.

If you are reading this card, you might have deciphered our secret code which of course is no more a "secret."

I can ease your desperation by the way. For sure you will counter attack my process of creating the 25th hour of time in the World of Time. I will make it easy for you.

If you want to know the secret of reversing the process of 25th hour, you are at the right place. The 3 Rings Anti Decoction Library. Use the decoction given at the back of this card and you will come across a fantastic thing where all the secrets lie. It also has the secret of generating 25th hour too. Try it out, you won't succeed in your motives. I have just mentioned it to you for a kind information. It's my duty to give a prior intimation to the Timekeeper. Anyways you won't succeed in all this.'

-Capvile

Robin was thunder-stuck. He was extremely baffled by this letter.

Rohan, Avni, Tara, Informer Spy and the Librarian all were looking at him.

He did not move himself in the air but gyrated his small fist in anger. But something clicked him at the very moment. 'Yes', he thought. 'I got the clue, at least. The consequences will be seen later.'

'Robin, what happened?' asked Tara frantically.

Avni and Rohan gathered some courage to ask – 'Reply, Robin'. They said it simultaneously.

Robin hastily spoke- 'Who gave you this card?'

'I don't know, few days ago when I reported to my work place, I found this envelope and a note along with it on my table,' replied Madam Lucy.

'The note said- Hand it over to Robin Spencer, the Timekeeper, whenever he comes here.'

'Is there any time gap between opening of the library and you reporting here?' asked Robin trying to figure out.

'Yes, of about half- an hour.'

'Do you have anything else to tell us?' asked Robin.

'Umm…No,' replied the Librarian concealingly.

'Rohan, Avni and Tara it's time to leave now. We had enough of our meeting with Madam Lucy,' said Robin in slightly inciteful tone.

'Informer Spy, you may also leave.'

Rohan, Avni and Tara were perplexed.

They followed Robin out of the library. Robin went through the air, straight without even turning once behind to check if the three were following him.

Informer Spy obeyed Robin. They went through the passage, down the staircase and out of the main entrance.

'Tara, without asking a question, please let's drive back to Royal Pine 66,' said Robin sounding tensed now. His mood kept changing constantly from being thoughtful to getting enraged or tensed.

Tara nodded her head. But she was extremely confused. 'What was written in the card?'

She predicted from Robin's behaviour that probably it was from Capvile. It had something to do with 25th hour. Her brain could think only this much for now. Rohan and Avni kept whispering to each other about all that happened on their way back.

They drove back home. 'Robin, now you must tell us everything,' said Tara banging the car key on sofa table of the drawing room. It was about to be noon when they reached. Mrs Chauhan was as well present for the discussion with utmost curiosity.

'I will narrate whatever happened and what we did from the beginning so that Mrs Chauhan comes to know about the exact scenario,' said Robin in a firm tone.

Mrs Chauhan listened to the incidence intently. 'Hmm...things are going to get complicated,' she said staring at the car key kept on the table after listening to whatever had happened. Robin had narrated everything including the card's content.

'What to do now, Robin?' asked Avni.

'You have the card, right? Just read the decoction aloud.'

'I will, Avni. But enough of stress for now. Let's have lunch. I need some energy to think. I won't take any wrong decision in a hurry,' replied Robin. He took out the decoction pouch from his upper circular portion where the digit '12' was written on his forehead. He quickly transformed into human. 'Mrs Chauhan, what's there for lunch today? I am extremely hungry,' he said, approaching the dining table.

'Stuffed parathas along with steamed rice for the main course,' replied Mrs Chauhan as she went inside the kitchen.

'Starter?' asked Robin.

'Sweet corn soup,' was the reply from inside.

'Dessert?' he asked

'Custard.'

'My word! The dishes are so similar,' said Avni to Tara as they settled on the dining chairs. 'We eat this on our planet as well.'

Tara smiled. 'Of course, our planet is invisibly present on Earth. Just the difference is that you don't have a Timekeeper and neither of you can use decoctions. Rest all things are similar.'

Mrs Chauhan served them with a sumptuous lunch. Everyone devoured it mindfully and no one talked about Capvile and his Card of Intimation. Robin enjoyed it thoroughly and while savouring steamed rice and curry he said- 'We have so many tasks to be finished and so much stress to handle. But the me time should never be dedicated to any of these but to our self. That is the 17th rule of yours, dear?' said Mrs Chauhan who was also sitting with them for the great lunch.

'Yes, obviously. It's written in my books,' replied Robin smilingly.

'17th rule? How many rules have you written?' asked Rohan as he poured a bowl of curry on his rice plate.

'And I was waiting for a question from your Rohan. Yes, it's my 17th rule. Actually, I have created, two hundred and fifteen rules of time,' said Robin now savouring the custard, even though his rice and curry plate was half finished.

'Please finish your rice first, Robin. Custard is for dessert,' said Tara reminding him of his mistake.

'There is no rule for that Tara,' replied Avni giggling. Mrs Chauhan smiled.

Royal Pine 66's atmosphere was quite tranquil. Everyone was eating wholeheartedly, as Robin was actually calm, others were also happy to see that. But something started lurking in Robin's mind- 'What will happen further? What we going to do and how?'

The Timekeeper was in stress. Thinking of the consequences of 25th hour gave him all the stress. The additional hour was going to have a huge impact on the daily lives of the people, but in a wrong way as artificially created 25th hour would be menacing.

The after effects of 25th hour would definitely impact Robin Spencer too. But he was concerned about the World of Time and not himself.

Rohan observed Robin's expressions and realised that he pretended to be calm but actually his friend looked troubled. He wondered- 'Why the Timekeeper doesn't have answers to all these things? Why is he so stressed?'

He wanted to ask several questions to Robin Spencer but was unable to.

The Battle begins

After the lunch, on the bright Saturday afternoon, the weather was quite good. The sky was pristine white and there was a calmness in the air.

Robin was drawing some detailed- 'Time Graphs,' which had the statistics regarding people who respected time, were punctual, people who actually were mindful of what they did at certain time. Of course, it also had the graphs for people who didn't value time.

Rohan and Avni were listening to Robin's each and every word, as they were sitting in the large living room of Royal Pine 66, their usual place.

Tara was out at the *Victorious Aura* office for an urgent work.

Mrs Chauhan was at her friend's house.

Tara had planned a meeting at 3.30 pm in the afternoon where all four of them were going to execute their plan. A plan which would initiate the real battle between Capvile and Robin Spencer. Robin was in human manifestation. Meanwhile he explained the twins about his 'Time Graph' further as the discussion was left halfway yesterday when Tara received the call from Informer Spy.

'I must say that time is life,' said Robin Spencer moving his ink pen in the air, gesturing towards Rohan and Avni.

'Have you heard the phrase- 'If you respect time, it gives back happiness and satisfaction ten times greater?'

'Phrases on World of Time and Earth won't be same right?' asked Avni. 'But we agree with what you said.'

'I didn't mean the exact phrase but try to understand its meaning deeply,' said Robin. 'Listen to me carefully, both of you. Time is a resource by which you are totally bound. You waste it, you lose it. You value it, you earn everything.'

'Robin, I had something to ask,' said Avni scratching her forehead. 'Go ahead,' was the reply.

'If someone is tampering with a resource so natural and superlative that is time, how can one be successful? Definitely that would cost the person heavily,' said Avni.

'And we believe in all this but not people like Capvile,' replied Robin, rolling that parchment of paper in his hand. He got up from his chair and started pacing here and there in the living room. 'The thing is that we don't know what is he doing and thinking to achieve that. He is a terrible alchemist.'

Rohan interrupted in between saying – 'The Card Robin, what about the Card? I am getting pretty impatient to unveil the secret decoction given in it. You did not read it at that time and neither of us were let to read...'

Robin stopped and stared at Rohan.

'You lack patience a lot,' he said. 'You very well know that once Tara comes, I am going to discuss the entire outline of our further mission.'

'Do you know Robin? Rohan is very impatient in studies as well,' said Avni changing the topic as she reckoned that two will start arguing unnecessarily. 'He cannot study for the more than fifteen minutes. But now we don't even get to study that much. We miss the school fun... our studies too, surprisingly,' said Avni suddenly getting nostalgic. 'We used to have so much fun back at home with our beloved cat. Our sincere and disciplined sister Akriti and of course – mom and dad.'

Rohan went towards her and put his arms around her shoulder. 'Even I am missing it all.'

'Well, your minds are connected with your twin counterparts. You can definitely think of them to know what's going there,' said Robin leaning forward on the dining table chair. 'Anyways it's just a matter of few days then you will be back at home again.'

Rohan wiped his tears and said – 'Means do you reckon that our missions and tasks will continue ahead in future?'

Robin smiled.

'They are always on, Rohan,' said Robin. The Timekeeper never rests. It is just that I found my friends again and until that I was on missions only with Tara.'

'Mention my name and I am here,' said Tara suddenly entering through the ajar main door of the house. 'Hope I am not much late.' She went straight towards a painting hanging on the wall behind the wooden work desk. The painting was of four different timepieces showing time of Northern, Eastern, Western and Southern cities of World of Time. She straightened the tilted painting and asked them to quickly gather at Golden Library.

'Follow me to the Golden Library upstairs. My personal work place and favourite too,' she said, whispering the last few words to herself. They went upstairs.

'Without wasting time, let's speak short sentences or more precisely, just say the most significant words required,' said Robin settling down on the leather chair which he had created using his decoction.

Everyone nodded their heads in agreement. Avni and Rohan made their minds to contribute to this paramount discussion, sincerely.

'The card, Robin,' said Tara.

'Yes,' he replied.

Robin quickly presented the card on the table from his pocket, in front of others. He flipped it and the backside was visible. There was a thick silver strip pasted horizontally and something was written below it, in dark red (but in small letters)-

'Scratch it with a coin.'

Robin did the needful. He took out a coin from his pocket and scratched it. Avni observed the big sized coin in his hand, surprisingly it had the imprint of Robin's timepiece manifestation.

'Are you the President of World of Time, Robin?' asked Avni.

'No', he replied firmly scratching the thick strip.

'Speak what is significant, Avni!' said Rohan and gestured towards her to keep mum.

The words under the silver patch were readable now.

'Can't believe this,' said Robin spencer getting up from his chair wearing a stupefied look on his face. 'Impossible.'

'What is it, just show it to me,' said Tara crossing the table and going on the other side to the read the card's backside.

Avni and Rohan leaned ahead to read too. 'What's is this?' asked Rohan who felt confused as he did not understand what was written.

Robin slammed the Card of Intimation on the table.

'How did I even expect that Capvile will mention the solution directly. There's a trick behind every step of that man!'

'Robin, speak what is significant. Keep your anger aside and explain what this means... Whatever is written on card,' said Tara almost losing her patience.

'He hasn't mentioned any decoction rather my vault number and its key,' he replied.

'Your vault number?'

'What's that?'

Robin took a deep breath and spoke-

'I have twenty-four vaults secretly protected in the sixth Main-square of Decoction factory. Those are secret as they contain extremely important possessions of the Timekeeper that's me. Nobody knows about the vault possessions except me. The password is supposed to be with no one except me. Now the fact is that they are no more a secret.'

Rohan, Avni and Tara looked flabbergasted. 'Twenty-Four secret vaults of the Timekeeper. What an amazing thing!' thought Avni. But a concern arose in her mind- Capvile had unveiled the secret. He had found about these twenty-four vaults.

Robin narrated and described his twenty-four vaults to Tara, Avni and Rohan.

'Robin let's go back to the Decoction Factory and visit sixth Main-square. It's too late to wait now. We must make quick movements,' said Tara.

'Of course, I must find out, how my Vault 20:07 was tampered,' replied Robin.

Vault 20:07, it seemed very strange. Avni and Rohan had heard every bit of Robin's story but the name 20:07 seemed like seven minutes past eight in the evening.

They were inching closer to their mission's significant level and nothing could disturb them.

Vault 20:07

They started off in their car again, towards Decoction factory. They also informed Mrs Chauhan on phone regarding their re-visit to the factory. Robin was in timepiece manifestation, but he had planned to transform into human once they entered the black castle of the factory so that he won't be visibly vulnerable as timekeeper, as most of the people weren't aware of his human manifestation. His timepiece transformation was required for entrance at the factory.

Sixth Main-square, corner of the second floor of Black castle of the Decoction Factory. A stained white door was in the front. No lock and latch. It looked quite dirty from outside and had a middle partition just like the floor lifts have.

Avni, Tara and Rohan reckoned that it opened from the middle, manually but they weren't aware about Robin Spencer's intellectual ideas to handle such things. He took out his decoction pouch. 'Hold the pouch, Tara,' said the Timekeeper, holding his miniature glass and a rose petal in one hand and a red ink bottle in other. He put the rose petal in the glass, poured three drops of the red ink, mixed the two with a mini spoon.

'How does he even remember these decoctions?' whispered Avni to Rohan.

Robin splashed the red liquid of the glass on the door. It slid apart for the four to enter. To Tara, Rohan and Avni's surprise there was nothing behind the door. Completely empty and dark space. There was no window for light to penetrate, not even a small source of light.

'What's this, Robin?' asked Tara.

'What will you do next to surprise us?'

'A way to make things visible,' was the reply from Robin and he nodded rigorously.

Rohan made a strange crackling noise which drew everyone's attention.

'Umm... Sorry, that was just to check whether an echo is there...' he replied hastily.

Robin did not listen to what Rohan said. He took out a small torch from his pocket, switched it on and went inside the room and rest three followed him. Even though the torch was on, Avni tripped on something hard and stamped on Rohan's shoes. 'Oh no! Avni what are you doing, you stamped on my foot,' he said.

Tara was behind Avni and she too tripped because of that hard object. It wasn't visible as Robin had projected the torch's light on a piece of paper and nowhere else. She reckoned it as a stone by touching it with her foot again. 'It's a stone,' she said.

'Detective mind!' exclaimed Avni to Rohan. 'She recognised it in dark.'

Tara giggled at Avni's statement. Robin did some rigorous movement. He whirled round and round thrice by flashing the light on a cream-coloured paper. The dark room had transformed into virtual vault room.

Avni hugged Tara tightly astounded. 'Fifteen thousand three hundred and sixth surprise,' she exclaimed. Tara looked at her and asked– 'what?'

'Those are the number of new inventions by Robin, according to me.'

Robin laughed. 'That's a pretty big number, Avni, well be ready for more. Before you ask, I will explain. This paper in my hand contains the image of my vault room. As I put torch upon it and whirled around thrice, you know what the result is now…'

The rest three gyrated their heads to have a look at the vault room.

Twenty-four lockers were piled up on each other at three adjacent walls of the room. Eight at each wall and four vaults piled up on another four.

The colour of all the vaults was dark blue but the virtual lockers had one unique feature. A horizontal opening was there on each locker as if it was meant for keys. The lockers really pleased Rohan and Avni as they smiled again and again, looking at the twenty-four vaults. They perceived it something really entertaining. Tara was carefully observing each vault with her detective eyes. 'Now without wasting time let us proceed ahead,' said Robin and he approached a smart computer screen on the left of the first vault on a dark blue virtual table.

Yes, in fact the smart computer wasn't real either. None of these objects had a solid appearance, they were particularly transparent and now the twins were very much interested in accessing the computer.

'Don't even think of touching the computer. Anyways it is a very different device, you can't operate it,' said Robin at once.

Rohan and Avni obeyed and Tara gave a short laugh.

'I have to access Vault 20:07 and for that this computer will provide a card from the screen of computer which has the password written on it,' said Robin looking tired of explaining everything.

'Does it generate a new password every time?' asked Tara in a typical detective voice with hands folded.

'No, until I change the password, it will produce cards of the same passwords,' replied Robin, operating the computer with right hand index finger as it recognized the touch of only one finger of Timekeeper, whether he was in human manifestation or his original state it didn't matter. Tara observed all this carefully as the computer asked various questions to Robin and he had to enter relevant answers.

First question popped up in a yellow box – full name of the Timekeeper?

Ans: -Robin Spencer.

Second pop up question in white box – which vault do you want to open?

Ans: -20:07.

Rest three were voice questions and The Timekeeper conveniently answered them only to leave the twins, Rohan and Avni even more confused and bemused with imperative range of questions- 'How does Robin have so many peculiar possessions which actually act according to Robin?'

But they chose to remain silent as Robin won't be interested to answer. Tara had finished her careful examination of the smart device and whatever Robin had done as a formality to get the vault open.

'You have a very safe and security bound system, Robin and I still can't decipher how the cunning Capvile has construed all your significant security plan….' Said Tara still standing with folded hands at the same position without moving and inch.

The screen of the smart computer produced a card from the very centre of it, Robin collected it and phlegmatically answered- 'I knew you will definitely observe everything. I am going with the flow not thinking much regarding how Capvile did this. Rather step by step process will benefit all of us at this point of time. By the way, I am pretty sure, that we will meet Capvile very soon.'

Rohan and Avni glanced at each other and nodded their heads. Tara did not react at all, rather stayed calm.

'I am going to insert the password correctly in to the Vault 20:07,' said Robin in a slightly nervous tone.

'I don't know what kind of new mystery awaits ahead, but we have to proceed in a way so that we can trick Capvile at any step. He will try to trap us in several ways and what is required from us?'

'Alertness, smart work and instant strategy making,' answered Avni which rendered everyone amazed for such a smart answer.

'That's brilliant Avni, how do you know these three principles are must for being a detective,' said Tara sounding curious to know.

'I read a few suspense-thriller books which involved detectives as the protagonist,' she replied.

'Do you read books? I did not know that,' said Rohan and he laughed.

'I think those are the only books she has read till now,' said Robin approaching the group of vaults at right wall of the room.

'Well Robin, you are so accurate in understanding things,' said Avni.

Rohan laughed heartily. Tara just smiled.

Robin was about to tell the password of 20:07. 'Let me tell you the password…'

Tara interrupted him and said– 'just show the card to us, do not say anything loudly, even the walls have ears.'

Robin agreed and showed the card. 'ADSHI#12$Time@ROB-SPEN' was written in bold letters.

'How could Capvile even decipher such a strong password? Robin, he's got some extra-ordinary talent or something special…,' said Rohan.

'It's a very complex password….' muttered an awestruck Tara. 'But the latter half of it is understandable to me.'

'Well, let's insert it now into the Vault 20:07,' said Robin and did not reply Rohan for his question.

He closed his eyes and smiled. Then he inserted the password card into Vault 20:07 situated near the centre wall at the right bottom. The vault accepted the card, made a strange sound and opened with a bang.

The object inside the Vault 20:07 stunned Tara, Rohan and Avni. They stared at it for many seconds without uttering a word.

Robin grinned anxiously.

A violet coloured, medium sized ball like object was conveniently fit into Vault 20:07 and it possessed a remarkable auto-rotating feature. The violet ball like structure looked hard but shined beautifully and rotated in air. The sleek appearance of the fancy object was liked by Avni instantly.

'Robin, this round object looks solid and it may contain some fingerprints as well if someone has touched it. Rest all things are virtual here,' said Tara in her usual detective voice and hands folded.

'Do you want to test this object? Do you really think Capvile will do such a mistake?' said Robin pointing out at the rotating violet object. 'Anyways Tara, no one can touch this apart from me.'

'Then how Capvile has ...'

'He's got other ways, I reckon,' replied Robin. 'To do the blunder.'

Something was going on in Robin's mind.

'And how did you change your opinion suddenly?' asked Tara, still hands folded. 'Up till now, you were worried about the fact that how Capvile has accessed your Vault 20:07.'

Even the twins were surprised to hear the change of opinion.

'After inspecting Purple Maglet with my eyes, I had to change my opinion,' said Robin.

'So, this is called Purple Maglet,' said Rohan. 'Such a childish name for such a cool object!'

Avni too did not like the name and made a face to convey her dislike. Robin gave a cold look to Rohan.

'What kind of inspection? Asked Tara taking out a magnifying glass from her long overcoat pocket. 'Hold the object in your hand and let me inspect then, I want to see!'

Robin took the Purple Maglet in his hand and it stopped rotating.

'The Purple Maglet changes its colour if someone touches it and nothing has happened to it. I am glad.'

'You need not inspect Tara. Trust me. The Purple Maglet contains the secret of the Timekeeper's birth, name and the human manifestation,' said Robin rubbing his palm on the sleek violet object.

Rohan and Avni were jolted. Mouths opened; eyes widened.

Tara knew about Robin's mystery but she wasn't aware about the violet-coloured object and the possession inside it.

'And what's the secret?' asked Rohan raising his eyebrows.

'Not now, Rohan. You both will come to know about it at the right time,' said Tara patting his back.

'No...' he said in annoyance. Avni got disappointed too.

'The button here above the Purple Maglet once pressed opens up the object,' said Robin, smilingly.

'Robin, what about Capvile and his message for us? Why are you taking up things casually? We have less time,' said Tara sounding vexed. 'I am not interfering much because I believe that you will do your job without any flaw, but I am noticing that you are progressing too slowly. You need not explain us everything present here. We are running late I suppose,' she said with complete displeasure. 'I could have inspected and deciphered every step of this mission had you informed me before, but I have done very little because you are taking up the initiative.'

'Calm down, Tara,' said Avni looking surprised at Tara's sudden loss of temper.

'Tara,' said Robin calmly and paused for a second or two. 'Its six in the evening and now Capvile can't alter the time. How much ever great alchemist he must be, but he can't experiment with decoctions or any chemicals to alter time after six in the evening and before twelve at midnight. It's a special blessing for the Timekeeper of this planet. Neither did he do anything before six as nothing happened to me and any changes in my outer appearance means the 25th hour is in process. But still I want to find out the exact trick Capvile has played and yes, I can see a card lying there besides the original position of my Purple Maglet...'

He spoke everything in one go.

'So, this wasn't there originally?' asked Rohan who heard every word of Robin mindfully.

'No,' said Robin and picked the card kept inside and placed his Purple Maglet back on the silver disc to render it rotating.

'Another card!' said Avni expressing her disappointment over finding another card. Tara regretted for having said so many things to the venerable Timekeeper and as she was about to say sorry, Robin said – 'No worries, Tara, it's alright if you scold me.' While saying this he was opening the white envelope in which the card was very safely kept. He didn't even have to look at Tara to know her regretful expressions. He instantly recognised what was on her mind. Tara felt good.

He read out aloud, whatever was written on the card-

'By the time, you receive this card I must have reached far, perhaps at the final stage of curating the 25th hour, dear Robin Spencer; our highly venerable Timekeeper. This card has been protected by decoction and for your info, insert this card inside the small opening of your Vault 20:07 and you will reach Hour Land, the place where 25th hour is almost ready to infuse itself in the Timekeeper, in the calm winds of every city and in the entire World of Time.'

P.S – 'Your three companions too must arrive at the place mentioned.'

The Venerable Alchemist

Capvile

Robin finished reading the letter. But this time he didn't feel enraged, neither his nerves fumed in indignance. Avni and Rohan were anxious and their heart pounded faster.

Tara cleared her throat and said – 'Robin, just go ahead.' She sounded very firm and determined.

Robin Spencer did the job. He stretched his hand and without disturbing the Purple Maglet inserted the card in the dark opening at the inside end of the Vault 20:07.

For a second, nothing happened but whatever occurred the next moment gave a vague view of the surrounding to the attendees of the large vault room. The next few seconds seemed to be complete darkness for them and they all four whirled around in the black surrounding. Robin was well aware of this but the other three were highly panicked and befuddled.

The darkness transformed into light slowly. Things came into view clearly and the confusion blended with panic, suddenly changed into extreme amazement. They were transferred to a different place. A room which was illuminated by the natural light from the only window which was well decorated with a nice shiny curtain, slit apart and a small plant pot kept at the window and peculiarly, rest of the room was empty. No furniture, except a door which was closed. 'Hour Land, isn't it?' said Avni glancing at Robin.

'Yes, but it seems that we have entered some house which I suppose is sea facing,' replied Robin. 'Look outside, we are at Spencer Sea. The sea looks calmer today.'

'Named after you, I see,' said Rohan nodding his head.

'But whose house, is it? Where are we?' asked Tara shaking Robin by his shoulders.

The door opened. A tall figure appeared with a hat and hands in the pocket of his long grey overcoat. His face was highly dislikeable. There was a shrewdness in his eyes and the pointed nose gave a feel of an antagonist entering a movie.

'Welcome to the great house of an outstanding alchemist,' said the person in a sharp voice.

The Cryptogram

That was not Capvile, but his younger brother- Junior Capvile.

Initially the twins mistook him as Capvile but then they remembered the video shown to them earlier by Robin and Tara in which Capvile's face was visible and it was even more cunning and evil than his younger brother's face. Avni exchanged a look with Rohan.

'That means Capvile has invited us to his house, feeling quite grateful,' said Robin standing with hands folded and wearing a fierce look on the face.

'I am equally grateful to meet Sir Robin Spencer, that too in his human manifestation,' said the evil faced, stepping inside the room.

'What does Capvile intend to do now? Why are we here?' said Robin.

'Calm down, Sir! My brother has instructed to escort our esteemed guests to the drawing room, sir,' he replied.

'I wonder how does your cunning brother track our whereabouts?'

'All answers,' said Junior Capvile putting his skinny hands in the overcoat of pocket, 'will be given in drawing room.'

'Come on Sir, don't waste time, it is very precious. Follow me.'

He gave a sharp look to Tara and marched out of the room.

The wise group of four followed him. They observed everything around. The empty room was the corner most one and many other rooms were present on left and they were walking through a long passage which had a different flooring.

On the right instead of low height railings, there were large glass shields which blocked the view of the rest of the house.

They turned at a point and walked again. In between the space of two rooms, paintings had been put up which were complex and non-understandable just like Capvile. Rohan and Avni didn't like being here. There was a strange smell in the air of the house which could easily render the mind dull and irritated. They walked more and finally a staircase was visible and everyone descended down.

Robin and Tara were extremely watchful of the enigmatic surroundings. Now as they descended down, the enormous living room came into view which was highly lavish and luxurious. They were absolutely spellbound and had assumed the house to be a palace as it looked so. The walls were full of similar complex paintings and the sofa was designed uniquely. There were large artefacts everywhere and small flower pots which had some ethereal blue and green feathers instead of flowers.

'Our wonderful guests have finally arrived,' said a voice, but none of the four could see anyone speaking as apart from them only Junior Capvile was present who was conveniently and comfortably smiling with a nasty expression and the voice heard few seconds ago was not husky like Junior Capvile's voice tone.

It was rather extremely dry and unpleasant. But Robin recognized the voice.

'Capvile, do not entertain us with your adroit tactics!' said Robin who was now about to be in a terrible mood.

'Hmm.. desperation is a nasty thing,' replied Capvile and he appeared in a sitting position on the leather sofa. He had his finger pressed on a blue button situated on the hand resting area of the large royal blue coloured couch.

'Dear Robin, your desperation may land you in trouble,' said Capvile removing his sunglasses which made his deep blue and extremely deceptive eyes visible to the guests.

Tara, Rohan and Avni exchanged startled looks. He paused and threw a nasty look at everyone. He had a heavy black fur coat which he was flaunting by drawing it closer to himself, a black cap which had his name printed in white, stylishly; pointed black shoes, eight rings in four of his fingers of both hands studded with vivid and attractive stones, a face with sharp jaw line, pointed nose, baggy and swollen eyes which looked terrible due the extreme dark circles.

All his features and his presence gave negative vibes to the four.

Tara returned an equally cunning look to Capvile and said – 'Answers, Capvile. I want to know them.'

'Ah…the not so experienced detective, Tara, the intelligent daughter of the perspicacious and pragmatic Journalist- Mr Ajay,' he said. 'You do not even possess a certified authority of being a detective. So do not order me to do things as if you are more powerful than me,' said Capvile cleaning his sunglasses. Tara was extensively enraged.

'Capvile not a word more!' said Robin. 'Straight forward answers only.'

'And why do you think I will answer? You're not so important to me. What presently matters to me is the inception of 25th hour,' he replied.

'Five and a half hours from here on and the 25th hour will be created. Once done, it will be touted as the greatest invention by a human in this world. Even you will accept that Robin,' he said.

'You should have been a little careful Robin,' he continued inspecting the long nails of his fingers. 'While operating your secret vault room.'

Robin widened his eyes and raised his eyebrows.

'May be someone secretly and invisibly observed what you did, deciphered all your passwords without your consent. Some people have the power to be invisible,' he said with a cunning smile.

Robin understood that his ultra security decoction for the vault room had been decrypted. Capvile had outsmarted the Timekeeper.

'I have a task for you, Robin by the way,' said Capvile.

'A hard challenge, rather,' he confirmed.

'The 25th hour is brewing up currently in a glass jar kept in a room. If you get the right anti-decoction, you can still save yourselves from the artificially created hour.'

He got up from his seat and walked around slowly. 'Let's make this casual meeting between us an intense one. I really wish to play a Cryptogram game with you Robin. Shall we?' He stared at the paper weight on table while speaking.

'Well, Capvile, I am always ready,' replied Robin.

Rohan glanced at Robin out of dissatisfaction. He thought- 'Why did he agree upon this? If Capvile manipulated then?'

'Excellent, Robin,' said Capvile putting his hand on Robin's back. The latter stared at Cavpile with a serious look.

'One Cryptogram and one answer of the correct anti-decoction ingredients to reverse the process of 25th hour,' said Capvile.

'My younger brother will ask you the most complex Cryptogram, which have to answer.'

Junior Capvile was smiling slyly leaning at the large orange wall in the room.

'Give me the privilege to ask the Cryptogram sir,' said a voice and the person appeared from the main entrance door which was half open.

Tara, Rohan and Avni were dumbstruck.

The person who came in rendered them speechless. But Robin didn't seem surprised.

'Informer Spy!' said Avni.

'He betrayed us!'

Rohan fumed with extreme anger. 'You cheat! How did you even think of betraying the Timekeeper? He asked.

Tara couldn't believe this. She was highly taken aback. Informer Spy used to sneak all the secret code words and messages to her for whatever few number of missions she had done till so far. He had informed the secret code 3RADLY as well. 'Reason; mention it,' she said clinching her fists and controlling the fury inside her which was about to burst.

'Of course, money, Tara. Capvile must have offered him tons,' said Robin very calmly. 'I already doubted this spy. I knew something was wrong.'

'Hmm...the Timekeeper is so smart,' said Informer Spy. But disappointingly Tara isn't that sharp witted.' He laughed heartily.

Robin, Tara, Avni and Rohan chose to be silent.

'Let's begin with the game now,' said Capvile settling down on the sofa. 'I am ready.'

'All this seems like a movie climax to me. I don't know why?' whispered Avni in Rohan's ears.

'Be serious Avni, this isn't a joke,' said Rohan out of displeasure.

'But these guys have made it a joke,' said Avni looking notably vexed and disappointed. She raised her voice a little higher just to say- 'Asking Cryptogram is the new trouble you have planned. Seriously you guys have lost your mind to disrespect the Timekeeper. Isn't it? Answer the Cryptogram, get the right anti-decoction and stop the formation of 25th hour. That is what you demanded right Capvile? How can you even think of taking the Timekeeper for granted? Robin Spencer is the supreme power, how much ever great invention you might think of manifesting, I have an ultimate and final statement to give- Mr Capvile. YOU WON'T SUCCEED IN THE INCEPTION OF THE 25TH HOUR.'

Tara and Rohan grinned a little and their eyes showed how satisfied they felt on Avni's long yet correct verdict.

Robin stood silent staring at Capvile.

Capvile was disturbed and enraged. 'I did not ask for your statement little girl. The 25th hour is already in the making and I am pretty confident on my invention unless Robin answers the anti-decoction Cryptogram right.' He took the paper weight kept on table and rotated it vigorously. 'But brother, he won't be able to answer. The unconventional Cryptogram is difficult to understand for any normal being except you and me,' said Junior Capvile

Robin seemed tranquil and composed. Tara observed his behaviour and thought that something is going on in Robin's mind. 'Has he found a solution for Capvile's blunder?' She thought.

'Very soon, the 25th hour will be born,' said Robin calmly. 'And I have accepted the fact that it will severely affect me which I need to tolerate. It will instil a lot of changes in my Timepiece manifestation, but won't complain. I will try to solve the Cryptogram as well, let me try.'

'Robin!' said Rohan out of excessive astonishment. Tara and Avni shared a similar expression.

The Timekeeper did not say a word ahead.

'The Cryptogram, Junior,' said Capvile with distrust and suspicion over Robin's statement.

Informer Spy too suspected him but remained silent with folded hands and screwed up face.

'Robin, do you really want to get entertained with some rubbish Cryptogram? Avoid this stupid game, suggested Tara. 'Find some solution.'

'An alchemist with great inventions doesn't entertain anyone with rubbish stuff, detective Tara,' said Capvile.

'Rohan, shall we try to read his mind to know the anti-decoction for the reversal of the 25th hour?' asked Avni in a low whisper.

'We can make use of our special talent.'

'I could hear that,' said Capvile. 'You can't read my mind, dear children and that's because of my special invention. It's a secret between me and my brother.'

'Oh no!' said the twins together.

'I want to know, Capvile, about how the 25th hour is in inception. I will answer the Cryptogram at same place.'

'Sure Sir, why not,' said Capvile in a very calm voice, playing with the same glass paper weight

Tara observed that the paper weight in his hand wasn't an ordinary one. It was rectangular in shape, made of glass, it consisted sand and two glistening stones inside it.

Capvile made his way towards a room under the spiral staircase. Rest followed him as well.

'And here is my invention in inception,' said Capvile standing near a wooden table on which there was a circular jar and a red liquid was boiling producing bubbles.

'I am curious Cavpile, to know the very significant process about the inception of 25th hour. How did you extract this information?' asked Tara examining the jar closely.

'Well, it's the result of my tenacious and consistent experimentation with hundreds of timepieces,' said Capvile leaning on the table craning his head into the jar. 'I need not extract any knowledge from somewhere else, it's my own invention. If we introspect our minds, we will extract something great that's what I learnt.'

'That's a fantastic learning Capvile but you are using it wrongly,' said Tara in a firm tone.

Capvile lifted his head up just to give an angry stare. That was quite arrogant,' he said.

'You deserve it,' replied Tara Savagely.

Rohan and Avni tried hiding their laughter.

'And yes the, Decoction Factory has been of great help,' said Capvile.

'Contradictory statements,' said Rohan confidently. 'I need not extract knowledge from somewhere else, this is what you said previously.'

'I want the Cryptogram, Capvile, as per your challenge. I need to decipher the anti-decoction,' said Robin staring at the glass jar which was about to change his fate as Timekeeper.

Informer Spy, the betrayer was desperate to do the job. He and Junior Capvile so far chose to be silent spectators, just to enjoy the conversations between the opposite parties.

Robin was, for some reasons, quite calm and his calmness looked weird to Tara.

Any of the statements from Capvile or whatever he blithered did not agitate the Timekeeper.

If Capvile succeeded in his intentions, 'World of Time' was to face repercussions. Robin would have to undergo a lot of changes in outer appearance and the artificial hour would be intolerable for him. The blue sky would change colours frequently and the rivers, seas and oceans would be far too aggressive than imaginable.

The desperate Informer Spy blithered out something, in a weird manner.

'Terrible hostility with water, we are three in number, difficult to decipher, guess it right to avoid the blunder,' said Informer Spy.

Capvile and his brother stared at him.

'You call this a Cryptogram?' said Tara, annoyed with Informer Spy.

'There may be hundreds of things which do not mix with water or cannot tolerate water,' said Avni. 'I thought so before, that this entire brainless gang is playing some tricks and fooling us with something rubbish.'

'Thanks for the adjective, little girl,' said Capvile. 'But Informer, you weren't needed here to blither out like this.'

On the other hand, within a flash of seconds, Robin sipped a decoction and transformed into Timekeeper.

What he did the next moment left everyone gobsmacked and open mouthed. 'NO…' shouted Capvile.

Robin Spencer snatched the glass paper weight from Capvile's hand and put it in the glass jar in which the decoction was brewing up.

'My job was to spoil your job and its done!' said Robin with a wide grin.

Capvile couldn't believe his eyes. The boiling decoction suddenly changed its colour to dark green and the paper weight floating inside was sinking down making the fusion of chemicals throw flashes of green smoke in the air.

The Exact Story

The hard experimentation of Capvile had fortunately failed. The green smoke indicated that.

The alchemist's eyes turned red in anger. He stared at the jar without blinking for quite a few seconds. It seemed as if he was lost for words.

Tara, Avni, Rohan and even Junior Capvile couldn't understand how Robin did all that and they looked flummoxed, no doubt.

'Robin, how did you know that?' asked Tara with a slight side smile and her face revealed a satisfaction.

'Robin Spencer and Informer Spy, destroyed my invention. These two spoiled my dream of becoming the greatest alchemist in the World of Time,' said Capvile clinching his fists, still staring at the jar. 'Informer Spy, you betrayed me!'

'Wait, what?' asked Avni and Rohan together in amazement.

'Of course, Capvile, I am always at service for the Timekeeper. Not For YOU,' said Informer Spy.

'Alright, let me make a guess,' said Tara folding her hands. 'Robin and Informer Spy knew about this glass paper weight being the anti-decoction. Informer Spy enunciated the Cryptogram in a simple way on purpose and

Robin was just finding a suitable time to do the job. Correct Robin?'

'Wait, what?' said Avni and Rohan repeating the same again.

'Correct, Tara. Now let me narrate the entire and exact story,' said Robin. 'An Alchemist who has great inventions to his name including some decoction ingredients, went as overconfident and crazy as he could quite a few years ago. He targeted the time next, read a book written by me named- *History of the twenty-four hours of time*. Thought of manifesting 25th hour. But Robin Spencer was aware of it. Informer Spy being a certified spy had the right to investigate in his own ways. He secretly passed on the information to me in the Vault Room today about his anti-decoction and that is how I was confident to destroy your ambition.' He paused and moved above in the air towards Informer Spy in his timepiece manifestation.

'He pretended to work for you, but his loyalty is towards the Timekeeper,' said Robin, giving a sly smile to Capvile.

Capvile was speechless. The attitude and impertinence he carried reflected even more on his face after his failure.

Tara had mixed emotions at the very moment. She was quite happy that Capvile's experiment had failed but she was hurt about the fact that Robin had secretly asked Informer Spy to do the job.

'Robin why didn't you tell us about all this?' she asked.

Robin replied very calmly, 'Tara, I was afraid after we received Card of Intimation from Capvile that he might be closely spying on us with help of his team members. Although I had already appointed Informer Spy to pass on the secret information to me. I wanted to keep everything to myself because Capvile is the most unpredictable being. In the past he has ditched many great alchemists in different ways.'

Tara was still dissatisfied. Informer Spy was desperate to explain few things and while Robin finished his long speech, he spoke- 'You might be remembering; Tara I had mentioned about few mysterious people at Spooky Café and one of them was Junior Capvile. They were discussing about three Rings Anti Decoction Library (3 RADLY). How meticulously these stupid people had planned to trap Robin, misguiding him frequently and finally brought him here to proudly show how 25th hour was brewing. But as you might have observed Robin was quite clam and composed since he came to know about the anti-decoction.' He paused.

'Yes, right from the Vault Room, his behaviour changed,' said Tara.

'With the help of a special decoction, I connected my mind to Robin and as I had come to know about the secret anti-decoction ingredient, I told him immediately. Special decoction courtesy- the Timekeeper,' said Informer Spy with a satisfactory smile.

Robin Spencer gave a short laugh. Meanwhile Capvile suddenly looked at Junior Capvile exchanging some serious eye conversation.

Avni's question, however caught attention of the rest, hence no one observed whatever Capvile signalled at.

'I have a very crucial, significant, relevant, pertinent and paramount question which I didn't even think of at first,' she said.

'Go ahead,' said Robin.

'What was the guarantee that Capvile's decoction experiment would have succeeded? Experiments do fail and this one would have failed too without adding any anti-decoction. Nobody pointed this out and everyone seemed assured! Why?'

'For a shrewd brain like Capvile, I am always high on alert,' said Robin. 'You can always expect something big from a clever brain. That's what made me worried about 25th hour,' he continued.

Informer Spy nodded vigorously agreeing to Robin.

Tara meanwhile glanced at Capvile just to ensure that he isn't playing any tricks because his silence actually indicated something suspicious.

There was a moment of silence and then- 'Robin!' said Tara with an awestruck expression. She pointed out at Capvile and his brother.

'Goodness!'

'My Word!'

These were the words from Robin and Informer Spy. But Rohan and Avni couldn't understand beyond the fact that Capvile and Junior were standing still. They weren't moving at all.

'False pretence decoction!' said Robin as he approached Capvile's still appearance. He snatched a thin cylindrical steel stick from Capvile's hand and threw it away on the floor. He did the same with Junior Capvile.

'Capvile and his brother have escaped,' declared Robin. He continued ahead- 'It's just their outer self-standing here which is a false pretence. Thirty seconds of holding this decoction stick firmly, a person can escape from anywhere giving the others an illusion of their appearance.'

Avni and Rohan had their hands on mouth. Few moments of silence and the noise of sea waves splashing on the rocks could be clearly heard.

'Good gracious, now what Robin?' asked Rohan, perplexed and shocked. 'He is free to do anything, he might take a revenge sooner or later.'

'Well, I had expected something of this sort to happen,' said Robin, blinking his small eyes, which looked evidently calm through his timepiece manifestation. 'A mysterious human mind can never be deciphered correctly.'

'Robin, what if he does this all again? He can repeat the entire experiment,' said Tara.

'Not again, Tara. Never.' He replied.

'Look at the green smoke coming from the jar. In the World of Time, there is only one decoction ingredient which produces green smoke upon failing- a neon green cloud flower. It blooms only once in a hundred years and only one of its kind grows in the hills. As Capvile has already used one, you will find another flower hundred years later.'

'Facts!' said Informer Spy. 'Facts which only Robin Spencer knows!'

Everyone laughed.

'So, for, what business are we waiting now?' asked Tara, now looking quite cheerful. 'Let's go back. Capvile won't be back soon, even if he does, we will handle him,' she smiled.

'How to go back? Any decoction?' asked Avni who felt quite satisfied and relieved now.

'No, not required. We are in a sea-faced house of Hour Land, but the backyard of this house leads to the main road of this city,' said Informer Spy.

'Oh, I wasn't aware of it,' said Robin as he prepared his human manifestation decoction.

'What? You weren't aware?' said Rohan emphasizing on the word 'you'

'Not necessary that the Timekeeper should know everything,' replied Robin in a relaxed tone, now that all the stress and hustle was out of his way.

They left Capvile's house where all the blunder was about to happen but Timekeeper's shrewdness, Informer Spy's clever support, Tara's intellect, Rohan and Avni's support, proved to be above Capvile's nasty intentions.

They headed straight towards a taxi to get back to Clockhist city as it was quite a long distance between the two cities. The street lamps were on as it was nearly 9 pm at night and slowly a cool breeze had started to blow around so the taxi windows were very much closed.

Robin had taken the front seat and rest were at the back-seats in the taxi. All of them were extremely hungry and sleepy too so none of them uttered a word. But the visuals of last four to five hours flashed in their drowsy heads frequently.

While they were in taxi, Rohan and Avni pondered about a few things which remained unanswered to them. They simultaneously thought of asking Robin whatever lurked in their mind, once they were back at Royal Pine 66, Clockhist City.

The driver was too fast in driving the car and it sped up gradually as they were nearing Clockhist. The night sky was full of twinkling stars and the dazzling silver moon added to the magnificent beauty of the sky painted with black. Robin admitted its beauty with his calm smile as he felt better and satisfied. He didn't want to think about any of his missions, adventures and the difficulties he encountered since past few days. He felt relaxed.

After two hours, Royal Pine 66 arrived. The drowsy heads were welcomed by Mr and Mrs Chauhan.

'There is a smile on Robin's face, means mission is successful!' said Mrs Sunaina Chauhan, with a wide grin. She gave a warm hug to Tara, Rohan, Avni and Robin.

Tara hugged her dad too. 'Dad, I am glad that you are back!' she said.

'I am meeting you after ages, dear,' said Mr Chauhan looking overwhelmed and perhaps expressed his emotions after a long time since he is never much used to it. Informer Spy expressed astonishment over Mr Chauhan's behaviour.

At 11 pm, they all had little bit of curd rice as none of the mission attendees had dinner and they were hungry.

'Goodness, do you all eat curd rice here in World of Time as well?' asked Avni savouring the delicious combo.

'Of course, dear,' replied Tara.

'Well, it's a very odd time of having dinner, but this sumptuous dish will be dedicated to our anxious yet exciting mission. So, let's enjoy,' said Robin.

After filling up the empty stomachs, nobody was in a mood to converse further and every one straight away went to sleep.

'I don't have energy to travel to my house, now all I need is a nice, cozy and warm blanket and a pillow. I have handled that evil-minded Capvile enough…' said Informer Spy looking so sleepy and tired as if he would doze off on the dining table itself.

'You can occupy the guest room on first floor,' said Mr Chauhan glancing at the sleepy faces. 'And, rest of you, go off to sleep, will talk about the entire mission in the morning.'

Waking up enervated in the morning everyone gathered together for a good breakfast.

The entire living room witnessed bursts of laughter, high-five exchanges, making a delicate clattering sound of the breakfast plates.

Mrs Chauhan looked extremely happy, having served so many people with her deliciously cooked food and having justified here cooking passion after journalism. Tara was explaining the incident verbatim to her dad and mom. But the bursts of laughter were because of Informer Spy who was adding some humorous lines in between while munching on cheese sandwiches.

'Capvile was so confident with his experiment,' said Tara only to get interrupted by Informer Spy.

'That fathead couldn't even think anything else apart from experiment,' he said.

Tara was getting annoyed with the interruptions.

Robin looked too hungry but didn't forget to laugh for the occasional humours. He gulped down the juice in one go and Avni laughed at that.

The breakfast was over after some time and Mr Ajay was appreciating all the efforts put in by the team.

Tara even asked for breaking out this news through media- 'Dad, should we inform the public about all this and how Capvile fled?'

'No, Tara, Robin Spencer is the Timekeeper and has a universal image of the most revered being in our world. If people come to know about this Capvile blunder, many such fatheads with wrong intentions would go against Robin. We never know,' replied Mr Ajay Chauhan, sitting on the recliner beside sofa. 'Although the people have a right to know everything, but this scenario was different which shouldn't be let out.'

Robin nodded his head in agreement. Meanwhile Rohan was desperate to show some piece of paper to Robin in his hand.

Mr Ajay observed it and immediately asked – 'Rohan, what's in your hand? You seem desperate.'

'Yesterday before going to sleep, I prepared a set of unanswered questions which remain a mystery to me,' said Rohan unfolding the piece of paper. Avni knew, what was lurking in Rohan's mind.

'And tell me your questions, Rohan,' said Robin curiously.

'First, existence of World of Time, the exact location of it. Second, your human manifestation, how can you transform into a boy of my age? Third, how come everything in this world ranging from names to food are similar to our world? What is the mystery behind Avni and Rohan's connection with World of Time?'

He finished reading and everyone was silent for few seconds.

'World of Time exists invisibly on Earth; I will talk about the exact location at the right time. My birth and human transformation are a mystery for you all and a long story for me which I will enunciate very soon,' said Robin. 'World of Time is inspired by Earth hence the similarity in every case. Our ancestors knew everything about Earth and got influenced.'

'Alright,' replied Rohan.

'Last question- what was our role in this mission? Most of the things were done by you, Tara and Informer Spy, we both didn't do much apart from being spectators just like the time when we watch a match in stadium, without doing anything.'

'Rohan, when you are playing some sport in school competition your parents support you, isn't it? Hence you are assured of your performance with enough confidence.

Just relate it completely with our mission,' replied Robin with hands folded.

'Got it,' said Rohan with a slight smile.

Robin's face suddenly changed to a disappointed one as if something popped up in his mind, an unwanted thought.

'And now,' he said and paused for few seconds.

'And now, Rohan and Avni need to return back to their house,' he added further.

'Oh no!' said Tara and hugged the twins tightly as if she won't let them go.

'Human bond,' said Informer Spy nodding his head.

Mrs Chauhan stared at him as if to say- Aren't you a human yourself?'

There were a few warm hug exchanges between Mrs Chauhan and the twins, then again it was Tara and both of them.

'This is the right time to go, Robin, I don't want to, but yes, I can feel that our twin counterparts are in my room, planning for some school competition. It's the right time to exchange positions, said Rohan teary eyed.

Avni rubbed her teary eyes.

'But this is just for time being,' said Robin with his usual smile.

'You two are frequent visitors of our planet now. There will be countless missions and tasks coming up for which you both have to be ready. Then there are so may mysteries to be unravelled.'

'Cheer up everyone!' said Mr Chauhan patting Robin, Rohan and Avni on the back getting up from his chair.

The trinity smiled.

Robin had his TTSM ready in next few seconds and the three were at the entrance of TTSM.

'It was fun, we will meet soon,' said Tara. Her parents and Informer Spy nodded.

'Tara, we will miss you and everyone else,' said Avni. They waved at each other and then the TTSM was off on its journey.

After some, TTSM door opened in the room of Rohan. The room door was closed and hence nobody could even peep inside.

The twin counterparts looked surprised. They did not utter a word and Robin asked the four to have the anti-decoction liquid and when the actual twins opened their eyes, everything was back to normal.

'Rohan and Avni, I need to return back to Hill Tower now,' said Robin a in a low tone which did not sound firm at all, rather forced. 'My home, you know.'

'Yes,' replied the twins with a smile and tears in eyes.

'Enough of the tears, guys. This isn't a farewell, I am coming back on next Sunday,' he said hugging the twins together.

'Of course, Robin it will be fun meeting again. Let's play Cricket together on next Sunday. I Hope you know the sport!' said Avni.

'Yes, Avni, I know the sport,' said Robin and went inside the TTSM.

'See you, Robin,' said the twins together. Robin waved back. The TTSM disappeared. Robin Spencer was off on his journey.

Rohan looked at the wall clock, it was new, probably purchased by the twin counterparts. 'The time is little different here by a few hours,' said Avni.

'Let's go!' said Avni and the twins marched out of the room. 'It's been ages, since we met mom, dad, Akriti and Tulip!'

www.ingramcontent.com/pod-product-compliance
Lightning Source LLC
LaVergne TN
LVHW061614070526
838199LV00078B/7274